Melissa Cl[...]
worth[...]

A TAIL OF TWO MURDERS

Jackie finds a beautiful dog with a bullet wound in his leg . . . and, not much later, the dead body of her boss at the Rodgers U. film department. The cunning canine may be a big help in solving the crime. . . .

DOG COLLAR CRIME

Dog trainer and basset hound devotee Mel Sweeten is killed with a choke collar . . . and Jackie and Jake have to dig up the facts to find out whodunit. . . .

HOUNDED TO DEATH

Mayoral hopeful Morton Slake has the morals of an alley cat—but when his girlfriend is found dead, Jackie and Jake prove that every dog has his day. . . .

MORE MYSTERIES FROM THE BERKLEY PUBLISHING GROUP...

INSPECTOR KENWORTHY MYSTERIES: Scotland Yard's consummate master of investigation lets no one get away with murder. "In the best tradition of British detective fiction!" —*Boston Globe*

by John Buxton Hilton

HANGMAN'S TIDE
FATAL CURTAIN
PLAYGROUND OF DEATH
CRADLE OF CRIME
HOLIDAY FOR MURDER
LESSON IN MURDER

TWICE DEAD
RANSOM GAME
FOCUS ON CRIME
CORRIDORS OF GUILT
DEAD MAN'S PATH

DOG LOVER'S MYSTERIES STARRING JACKIE WALSH: She's starting a new life with her son and an ex-police dog named Jake...teaching film classes and solving crimes!

by Melissa Cleary

A TAIL OF TWO MURDERS
DOG COLLAR CRIME

HOUNDED TO DEATH

GARTH RYLAND MYSTERIES: Newsman Garth Ryland digs up the dirt in a serene small town—that isn't as peaceful as it looks..."A writer with real imagination!" —*The New York Times*

by John R. Riggs

HUNTING GROUND
HAUNT OF THE NIGHTINGALE
WOLF IN SHEEP'S CLOTHING

ONE MAN'S POISON
THE LAST LAUGH

CALEY BURKE, P.I., MYSTERIES: This California private investigator has a brand-new license, a gun in her purse, and a knack for solving even the trickiest cases!

by Bridget McKenna

MURDER BEACH

JACK HAGEE, P.I., MYSTERIES: Classic detective fiction with "raw vitality...Henderson is a born storyteller." —*Armchair Detective*

by C.J. Henderson

NO FREE LUNCH

FREDDIE O'NEAL, P.I., MYSTERIES: You can bet that this appealing Reno P.I. will get her man..."A winner." —Linda Grant

by Catherine Dain

LAY IT ON THE LINE

SING A SONG OF DEATH

SISTER FREVISSE MYSTERIES: Medieval mystery in the tradition of Ellis Peters...

by Margaret Frazer

THE NOVICE'S TALE

THE SERVANT'S TALE

HOUNDED TO DEATH

MELISSA CLEARY

JOVE BOOKS, NEW YORK

If you purchased this book without a cover, you should be aware that this book is stolen property. It was reported as "unsold and destroyed" to the publisher, and neither the author nor the publisher has received any payment for this "stripped book."

HOUNDED TO DEATH

A Jove Book / published by arrangement with
the author

PRINTING HISTORY
Jove edition / September 1993

All rights reserved.
Copyright © 1993 by Jove Publications, Inc.
This book may not be reproduced in whole or in part,
by mimeograph or any other means, without permission.
For information address: The Berkley Publishing Group,
200 Madison Avenue, New York, New York 10016.

ISBN: 0-515-11190-2

Jove Books are published by The Berkley Publishing Group,
200 Madison Avenue, New York, New York 10016.
The name "JOVE" and the "J" logo
are trademarks belonging to Jove Publications, Inc.

PRINTED IN THE UNITED STATES OF AMERICA

10 9 8 7 6 5 4 3 2 1

For Tyke and Will

CHAPTER 1

At her desk in the city room of the Palmer *Chronicle,* Marcella Jacobs punched the keys of her word processor in frustration.

"Damn!" she muttered as she tried one combination of letters after another. With each attempt, the same message was repeated on the screen: <BAD COMMAND OR FILE NAME>.

"Hey, Bingo," she called to her neighbor in the next cubicle. "Have you got a problem with retrieval today?"

"No." Stuart Allen kept typing at top speed, his long, thin fingers flying with a pockety-pockety noise across the plastic keypad. Bingo could type a hundred sixty words a minute. So he claimed. "No. You lose another story, Jacobs?"

"Oh, shut up," replied Marcella, her irritation showing. Where had her file gone?

Stuart Allen—Bingo—was the one who always lost stories in the vast centralized filing system at the *Chronicle.* He was notoriously secretive, claiming that he wrote on sensitive issues that could touch off a recession or a stock-market crash. (His beat was the city's financial community.) He gave his stories code-names out of the Hardy Boys, with passwords that seemed like nothing more

1

than random combinations of letters and numbers. In fact, they were random combinations; hence the nickname "Bingo."

"Maybe it went to Editorial," said Bingo helpfully.

"No way." Marcella's voice had a most unusual whine in it today. "It's not due for another two weeks."

"Oh. Well, what do you care?"

"Shut up. It's a lot of work that's lost."

"What is it?"

"The profile of Morton Slake."

"Oh." Bingo looked up long enough to yawn widely. Then he laughed. "Probably the system rejected it. Too boring."

"Oh, shut up."

In spite of this momentary setback, Marcella Jacobs was pleased with herself. She had protested when the metropolitan editor had transferred her from the police beat to city government, considering local politics about as interesting as watching corn grow.

But in her profile of Morton Slake—the current president of the Palmer city council, who was running for mayor—she had found hints that there might be plenty of interesting muck to rake, if you could just get to the right sources.

The story as it stood wasn't all that exciting—Slake was depicted as just another politician, up to the usual politician's tricks, and filled with the deepest insincerity. But Marcella had hopes of spicing it up before the deadline—she was trying to track down a source, but so far she hadn't had much luck. That was okay—still two weeks to the deadline, and if she didn't get the dirt she was hoping for, the story would still work as written.

Slake's connections weren't all with the Jaycees and

the Boy Scouts. He was good at covering his tracks, but there was a very good chance that she could find some mob ties if she looked hard enough. That's what she was after. This bland profile was just the beginning. She didn't have the confirmation she needed yet, but she had developed an idea where to get it. After that, it would be a cakewalk. Morton Slake would have to look to his laurels.

Marcella had recently moved back to Palmer, her hometown, after an absence of fifteen years. She believed that one of the best ways to get to know a city was to know its cops, so on taking the job at the *Chronicle* she had asked to be assigned to the crime desk, a slot typically reserved for reporters still wet behind the ears. A few months covering liquor-store holdups, local homicides, bank robberies, and domestic disputes would give her the time and the opportunity to assess Palmer on her own. She would be able to make up her mind about the city, before the locals figured out that she was here, and that she could be a fierce ally or a dangerous enemy.

So far, Marcella Jacobs seemed to be the only person in Palmer who had really bothered with Morton Slake. To everyone else in town, he was more or less of a municipal fixture, like Beakins Park or the statue of John Marland. Marcella, however, had been observing this Palmer fixture with fresh eyes; and her gaze generally tended to be a suspicious one. In her first big assignment at the *Chronicle,* Marcella hoped to do what she had done before, in Philadelphia, with such devastating force. Marcella had put the pieces together and come up with the possibility that Morton Slake, as the saying went, wasn't quite as dumb as he looked.

But this morning, her story on Morton Slake was gone. The file had been dumped. Despite the carefully erected security system that Marcella had designed to keep out prying eyes, someone had found the access code. Someone had wiped out her story.

Marcella Jacobs was upset, but this was by no means a disaster. The piece had still needed a lot of rewriting, and she was only halfway through it. She had her notes at home, in a safe spot—and it was a sorry reporter who couldn't reconstruct a story. Marcella would be all right.

But she was most definitely intrigued by the file's disappearance. Before she jumped to conclusions, she would have to talk to Matt Hannover, the computer technician, to make sure. But she had used the CompuLink System for years, and knew its ins and outs pretty well. It looked to her like someone had penetrated the four-level password that had guarded the story. Politics as usual. She was glad her notes were under lock and key at home.

"Hey, Bingo," she called, grabbing for her pocketbook and her jacket.

"What?" Bingo answered sullenly. He wasn't known for his camaraderie.

"Know anybody who's got it in for me?"

"Hunh-uh," said Bingo. "Don't worry, you'll remember the password eventually. I always do."

"Right. Well, in case I don't, keep your ears open, will you? I think maybe I've been sabotaged." She headed out through the busy room into the hot, muggy August air.

"Sure," muttered Bingo, typing away. "They all say that."

In the offices of the city council, Morton Slake was combing his thick, wavy, black hair. Slake was a sturdily built man in his early fifties, barrel-chested, with a dark complexion and dark eyes. He had been running the Palmer City Council for nine years, and he was widely considered the favorite in the city's upcoming mayoral contest. A favorite—hell, he was a shoo-in.

His war chest was full to overflowing—not only was Slake well known and widely supported, he was also a millionaire in his own right, having made a fortune in commercial real estate. Technically, it was his wife who was the millionaire, but Slake had forgotten that long ago.

When he joined the city council, Slake had been instrumental in rewriting half of the city's zoning laws—necessary reforms that, by merest coincidence (he said), served to guarantee the commercial value of all the existing Slake properties for at least another two decades. He had downtown Palmer sewn up, and he didn't care what anybody thought about it. Zoning was zoning; could he help it if it worked out in his favor?

The competition in the election had at first seemed rather one-legged, and Slake's "Law and Order" ticket had promised to sail along virtually unchallenged. Slake's money and position made him almost impossible to challenge; moreover, he had a clean, solid record with the city council (with that one question mark about the zoning laws—but that was ages ago). There were few people who saw any reason to oppose him. The outgoing mayor had served three terms—the limit—and had given his full backing to Slake.

The only opposing candidate was Jane Bellamy, a forty-five-year-old professor of city planning and urban administration at Rodgers University. Slake had dismissed her with a chuckle. "A woman?" he had asked, disbelieving.

When one of his campaign counselors had pointed out that Jane Bellamy was also a Ph.D. in city planning, Slake had scoffed anew. But apparently he thought enough of the threat, back in April, to do some actual campaigning. He had adorned all of his commercial properties with huge bill-boards that read, "Those who can't do, teach." He thought that should take care of the matter.

Unfortunately, Slake's counselors told him that Bellamy hadn't given up; nor did she appear likely to do so. She was campaigning hard against the "Palmer machine politics"; Slake wanted to know what the hell was the matter with machine politics—the system had worked for years, hadn't it? But after a while Slake began to take the campaign personally. Bellamy, in Slake's words, had a "thing" about running against him. "What'd I ever do to that broad?" he was wont to complain, before comforting himself with a bromide: "She'll get hers."

This morning Jane Bellamy was once more on Slake's mind. "I don't think this election's going to be as easy as we thought, Timmy," Slake remarked to his young aide.

Tim Falloes, a lanky blond of thirty with a ready, full-lipped smile and a curiously unfocused gaze, held out Slake's suit jacket. "You see problems?" he asked deferentially, helping his burly boss into his coat.

"Well, I wouldn't say problems. But I sense sympathy for that Bellamy woman. From the university types, women, and other softies. I wish you could dig up something decent on her. Lovers?"

Falloes shook his head. "We looked. No go. Sticks to her husband."

"Kids? Delinquency, pot, failing in math?"

"Nope. Track team, student government."

Slake swore. "How about the husband, the lah-di-dah doctor. Malpractice? Drug connections? Anybody check out his prescription list lately?" Dick Bellamy was the chief of medicine at Marx-Wheeler Memorial Hospital, the largest in Palmer and widely respected nationwide.

"Nope. Clean. They think he's a god over there."

Slake swore again. "She's a good looker, that dame. Hard to believe she hasn't got a boyfriend. Maybe she's—uh—you know." He twiddled his fingers around in the air. "Boy, that would be great."

"No, we tried that one too. No luck."

"Keep at it, Timmy. Got to be something we can use." Slake adjusted his bright green silk tie and brushed away a few specks of dust from his sleeve. He glanced at his watch. "What time do the cameras roll?" He was giving his weekly televised press conference—a routine that the city council president had adopted as soon as he decided to run for mayor.

Falloes looked at his watch. "Five minutes."

"Good. Get me a drink, will you? And get Bambi on the phone. Tell her I'll see her for lunch at her place. As soon as I finish with public relations." Slake narrowed his eyes and smiled.

"Right."

Marcella Jacobs was quiet throughout the press conference, which was brief. This week's televised conference concerned a recent council vote about sewage regulations. Nobody in Palmer had dared complain to Slake about his abuse of free television time; it was, after all, standard campaign practice for most incumbent politicians, although few people would have taken advantage quite so brashly of this incumbent's edge. Marcella Jacobs, intensely bored by the topic, also felt that she had seen quite enough of Slake lately, over the course of seven or eight lengthy interviews.

This morning Slake often looked her way, curious at her silence; she smiled back. She had played the bimbo role well thus far—her long red-gold hair and her stunning figure were assets, she knew, in building up Slake's false impression of her. She wore sexy dresses to their interviews and let Slake draw his own conclusions—she knew what they would be. Slake was one of those men who thought they could control a woman by being agreeable. Morton Slake could be very agreeable to women when he chose. Many women even thought him handsome.

But Marcella Jacobs wasn't the kind of woman to fall for Morton Slake, agreeable or not. More than a few of her profile subjects in Philadelphia had learned about her the hard way, having assumed, like Slake, that a woman couldn't be beautiful and razor-sharp at the same time.

When the press conference was over, Marcella hurried down the long flight of marble stairs, through the main gilt-and-marble foyer of Palmer's City Hall. She needed to get right to work on reconstructing her story. Matt Hannover had said he would try to help find a ghost in the system, but Marcella Jacobs held out little hope of that. She would just have to write it all over again, and the sooner she got started the better.

She climbed into a well-worn blue Volkswagen bug and chugged off toward her small apartment, not far from the campus of Rodgers University. A native of Palmer and an alumna of Rodgers, Marcella Jacobs had found great comforts in the old neighborhood, after the disappointments and difficulties of her life in Philadelphia. It had been good to come home.

Marcella's apartment, a cozy little retreat with high ceilings, moldings, and a working fireplace, occupied the second floor of a century-old rowhouse. It was a stately building and, like the rest of the rowhouses on this small stretch of Cider Street, it had been beautifully restored by a developer whose specialty was historic preservation. It was a beautiful spot, and Marcella counted herself lucky to have found it.

She hurriedly mounted the marble stoop, let herself into the foyer, and took the indoor stairs two at a time. Even before she reached the apartment door, she had a strange sense that something was wrong. She hesitated a beat; then, with the willful curiosity that had shaped her career, she inserted the key in the lock and turned.

CHAPTER 2

"Come *on*, Mom!" urged young Peter Walsh, standing at the corner of Isabella Lane and Chestnut Street. A strong summer breeze, already heavy with the promise of coming thunderstorms despite the early hour, ruffled his reddish hair, and he bounced up and down, from one foot to another, impatient but trying not to show it. "Jake is really ready."

Jake—a large, powerfully built German shepherd, just starting to go gray around the muzzle—looked up briefly at the mention of his name. Jake didn't look particularly ready, or not ready, one way or another. The wind lifted and parted the long black fur at the center of his back, above his shoulders. He gazed upon his family mildly, from son to mother and back again. He looked forbearing and wise, really, more than anything, thought Jackie.

"Coming, Petey," shouted Jackie in response, but her voice was caught by the wind and carried off behind her.

The boy and the dog watched as Peter's mother, Jackie, made her way hurriedly down the narrow sidewalk on Isabella Lane to catch up with her son at the corner.

Jackie Walsh was in her late thirties. Young-looking and athletic, she had thick, long, chestnut-colored hair that blew wildly in this morning's wind. Her open features bore their habitual look of good humor and high spirits,. These were

11

qualities that Jackie, as the divorced mother of a ten-year-old boy, called upon steadily.

On this particularly blowy Saturday in early August, Jackie, Peter, and Jake were headed for Holcomb Park to play soccer with Isaac Cook, (Peter's best friend), and Isaac's parents. Jackie thought it looked like hurricane weather, and every moment seemed to threaten rain, but the boys had been planning this outing all week, and Jackie and Sarah—after a brief consultation this morning by telephone—had decided on their strategy. They would play for half an hour or so, and then the teams would head to Klinglehoffer's Kakes, a local bakeshop, for doughnuts and milk shakes and coffee. Nobody would complain about that.

To even out his team, Peter had invited a friend to play—a friend of the family. This was Lieutenant Michael McGowan, a detective on the Palmer police force, who had become something of a regular visitor of Peter's and Jackie's since their move to Palmer the year before. The circumstances of their initial acquaintance with McGowan weren't all that pleasant to contemplate—Jackie had first met him during the course of an investigation into a murder of one of her colleagues in the film department at Rodgers University. But since that time, McGowan had become more or less of a fixture in their lives. He was also divorced, and for a long time Jackie had suspected that there might be more than simple friendship behind his attentions to her and her son, but many months had passed, and McGowan had settled into playing a kindly, avuncular role with Jackie and Peter.

Jackie was relieved, although at some level she had to admit she was slightly disappointed as well. She had rather enjoyed the image of herself as the fiercely independent young mother, keeping the ardent suitors at bay while she established herself in her new life. It had been just about a year since she and Peter had returned to Palmer, without Cooper, Jackie's former husband.

Palmer was Jackie's hometown, a natural place in which to seek refuge when her marriage had dissolved. Her mother lived not too far away (not too close, either), and there were a few old friends still in town from high-school days. Before marrying Cooper Walsh, Jackie had briefly had a stint as an instructor of film history at Rodgers University, and by a stroke of pure luck she had managed to get her old job back.

She and Peter lived near school, in a once-seedy area that had recently begun to find its way up in the world. They had bought a small, two-story industrial building on Isabella Lane, and Jackie had carefully supervised the transformation of the raw space into a comfortable duplex loft, airy and welcoming and altogether different from the little suburban colonial house in Kingswood where her marriage had gone to pot.

At first Jackie had been worried about Peter—his father was still in Kingswood, more than an hour's drive away. But Peter had taken to city living like a duck to water. At the Downtown Arts School he had quickly made friends, and there were plenty of after-school activities—sports, dramatics, and art classes—to keep him happy and deeply occupied. He didn't seem to miss the suburbs much.

Well, Jackie would be the first to admit it: Kingswood was a particularly bland and enervating place. It was the kind of place that people aspired to; and once they had attained it, they never looked beyond their own little society. Or so it had seemed to Jackie, who had felt like a prisoner for the last four or five years of her married life. Mostly, the children went home after school to play Nintendo or to watch television. There weren't many organized activities that would challenge or broaden a child; the little boys and girls there were expected to proceed from a dull childhood into a duller adulthood.

Kingswood didn't have a theater or an amateur chamber group. The local library—small and scantily lined with books—was open only four mornings a week. There wasn't even a movie theater; the old Bijou had, predictably, given way before the compelling presence of a huge video-rental outlet. To see a first-run movie, you had to drive twenty-five minutes to a mall on the outskirts of Palmer, where you could choose from eight mindless features all playing simultaneously in the uncomfortable, thin-walled, badly constructed OctoPlex.

Being a grown-up in Kingswood had seemed to Jackie nothing but endless rounds of mediocre golf followed by mediocre meals at the Kingswood Country Club. This routine was highlighted by three or four big dinner-dances every year, events that kept most of the Kingswood ladies planning and anticipating throughout the four seasons of the year. Jackie didn't play golf, and she disliked dinner-dances. In Kingswood, she stuck out like a sore thumb.

Even so, Jackie would not have given up on Cooper, on their life together—she was not a quitter. She had been on the point of insisting that they move—but Cooper had made her getaway easy by taking up with a fellow golfer at the Country Club, a divorcée who, Jackie supposed, had rightly seen through the mismatch that their marriage had become. Jackie hadn't known how to make life in Kingswood exciting for Cooper; she had failed, she often admitted to herself, to meet this particular challenge. The golfing lady had met the challenge much better.

So everything had worked out for the best, it now seemed to Jackie. The only worry had been Peter, and in Palmer, Peter was flourishing as never before. Even Cooper had noticed, and approved wholeheartedly. Cooper, for his part, was much better suited to being a weekend father than a full-time family man. He liked to get in his games of racquetball every evening after leaving the small investment company where he had worked for fifteen years. He liked, after racquetball, to come home and eat a solitary dinner before the television, watching whatever sports he could find, and postponing or avoiding conversation. He didn't like to help Peter with his homework, or to talk about the day with his wife, or to do much of anything except work, play, and sleep. This life had made Jackie exceedingly tired; now everything was vastly improved. Cooper could be a lively and interested father for thirty-six hours every two weeks, but it wasn't easy for him to give more. Even Peter seemed to understand; he seemed to like his dad much better now—now that Cooper wasn't letting him down every evening.

Jackie and Peter and Jake arrived at Holcomb Park just as the Cook family turned up, coming from the other direction. Isaac had brought his soccer ball, a new one, and he and Peter rushed out to set up the goals and to do some fancy footwork, while the adults shivered and chattered under a tree. Within a few moments, Peter and Isaac had mapped out the playing field, and they called impatiently to the grown-ups to join them.

"We're waiting for Michael, Petey," said Jackie, who didn't mind the idea of a few moments' adult conversation before the match began.

Sarah Cook was an artist, and her husband Paul taught Spanish and Portuguese literature at Rodgers. Isaac was an only child, like Peter, and the two boys had been best friends since the day they met. Jackie sometimes couldn't believe her good fortune—that Peter's best friend should have such likable parents. She and Paul had a lot to talk about, one way and another, for university politics influ-

enced their lives deeply. And with Sarah, Jackie had found
a real affinity, of the kind that adults rarely discover with
new acquaintances. She and Sarah were friends. Over the
last year they had spent many late afternoons together,
while Peter and Isaac were playing, laughing and talking
and eating the homemade cookies that they had baked,
ostensibly, for the boys.

"So I hear you invited your policeman to play with us,
Jackie," said Paul Cook, hopping back and forth from one
foot to another to keep warm.

"He's not 'my' policeman, Paul," said Jackie evenly with
a smile. "He's just a friend."

Sarah poked her. "Mmm."

"Well, he sure helped you out with Jake," commented
Paul.

"That's true. I owe him for that one," said Jackie. The
history of Jake's arrival in their family was complicated.
Jake was an ex-police dog whose master had been murdered, but he had turned up at Jackie's house all on his
own, adopting her and Peter without ceremony. It was
only later on, when the dog's provenance became clear,
that Michael McGowan had taken action, helping Jackie
avoid the bureaucratic complications created by Palmer's
adoption process for animals retired from active service.

"Well, I'm curious to meet him. Inquiring minds want to
know," he added with a laugh.

Paul was being up-front about it, anyway. Sarah, Jackie
noticed, had carefully avoided being too inquisitive about
this morning's plans, although she, too, was undoubtedly
curious about Michael McGowan. All of Jackie's friends
were curious.

Last fall, when Jackie's colleague Philip Barger had been
murdered, she had helped McGowan solve the case—she
and Jake, to be precise. It was actually Jake who had

finally cornered the murderer. The investigation had been fascinating and terrifying all at once for Jackie, who had decided that she wasn't quite as intrepid as she would have liked to be when confronted with a riled-up murderer. But McGowan had been unstinting in his praise of both Jackie and Jake, insisting that without them he couldn't have solved the case.

Then, not long ago, a local dog trainer had died in mysterious circumstances. Once more, McGowan had found that his case rested on Jackie's enthusiastic if amateurish investigations into the facts surrounding the man's death. Her efforts, to be accurate, could never have taken place without Jake, who had provided a valuable entree into the rarefied world of professional dog trainers and championship dog shows.

Sarah Cook, having heard the details of the two cases, was naturally curious. What true friend wouldn't be?

In a few moments McGowan appeared, looking boyish and handsome in blue jeans and a dark blue jacket that matched his eyes. The wind ruffled his long, dark hair, and he jogged toward Jackie with an athletic ease that was admirable to see. Jackie made the introductions as Peter waved madly from the playing field. He was evidently eager to show McGowan off to Isaac.

"God, what miserable weather," McGowan complained, smiling at Jackie. "I hope Peter appreciates the effort I made to leave my bed for his sake."

"We all appreciate it, Michael," Jackie responded. They made their way onto the field. Peter ran up to McGowan and stood, looking happily up at him, a huge smile on his face.

"That's Isaac," said Peter, pointing.

"Hiya, Isaac," McGowan called. "I see you brought Jake," he added to Peter.

"Of *course*," said Peter, impatient. That was a silly

observation for a detective to make.

"We never go anywhere without him," said Jackie simply. It was more or less true.

"He's a great dog, isn't he?" McGowan gave Jake an admiring glance. For all his ten years, the dog was still lithe and powerful, impressive to look at.

"I'll say," commended Sarah Cook. "Isaac adores him too, even though he has three perfectly good dogs of his own."

"Three!" McGowan laughed and gave Sarah Cook an appreciative look. It wasn't just any woman who would encourage her son to have three dogs.

The three-on-three soccer game progressed smoothly, and Jackie, in spite of her usual caution, was beginning to wish that McGowan were more often a part of their lives in this friendly, everyday manner. Their friendship had developed under strenuous circumstances—for a murder investigation, no matter how interesting, is never a cozy affair. Jackie realized, as she watched McGowan make a skillful dodge around Paul Cook, that she enjoyed seeing him so relaxed. Most of the time they had spent together he was working, at some level or another. She liked him like this, and wanted the chance to see him more often in this way.

When the game was over—the Cooks had won, by three goals—the group headed for Klinglehoffer's Kakes, where they noisily took over the largest booth and ordered an entire strudel. Isaac, unable to contain himself any longer, began to grill McGowan on the ins and outs of detective work.

"Do you have to wear a gun?" he asked. Jackie had noticed Isaac glancing curiously, from time to time, at McGowan. Evidently he had been checking him out for a weapon.

"No, I don't have to," said McGowan, "but I sometimes do. It depends on where I'm going and what I'm doing."

"Like if you're chasing crooks or not?" asked Peter, by way of enlightening Isaac.

"More or less. If I'm chasing crooks who use guns. There are plenty of crooks who don't, you know."

"Collar criminals," said Isaac.

"Yeah—close. White-collar, we call them. People who embezzle money, or make a lot of shady deals on the stock market, or that kind of thing. Sometimes I work on cases like that."

"Oh." Isaac sounded disillusioned. "Well, what about Jake?"

"What *about* Jake?"

"I mean, he never chased white-collar guys, when he was a police dog."

"No," McGowan agreed solemnly. "No, his talents are better suited to the pursuit of more active crooks—drug dealers, holdup men, burglars. Oh—speaking of burglars—Jackie?"

"Yep?"

"You have a friend called Marcella Jacobs."

"Yes . . . oh, no, what's wrong?"

McGowan held up his hand. "Everything's fine. I ran into her yesterday, late in the day, down at the precinct house. Her apartment had been burgled."

"Oh, dear." Marcella's apartment wasn't far from Jackie and Peter's place. Jackie shook her head. Crime everywhere. She struggled to remind herself that the outwardly peaceful suburb of Kingswood had been just as bad—in fact, worse. "Poor Marcella. She just moved back to Palmer. She said Philadelphia was getting too rough."

"So she told me. You grew up together?"

Jackie nodded. "Same class, all the way through school."

Suddenly Jackie began to feel embarrassed. How had McGowan known they were friends? The only way was if Marcella had mentioned it. Jackie felt a blush coming on. Obviously, when McGowan introduced himself to her, Marcella must have said, "Oh, you're Jackie Walsh's cop," or something like that. Terrible, it was terrible to have people find out you'd been talking about them. Especially handsome, eligible men who were acting ambivalent toward you, and about whom you had not made up your mind. Jackie's face was a picture of dismay, which Sarah Cook seemed to understand and find amusing.

McGowan didn't appear to notice Jackie's consternation; he was stirring his coffee thoughtfully. "She mentioned that she knew you—seemed to think it would help her get special attention from the detective force."

"That name is familiar," put in Paul Cook. "Isn't she a reporter for the *Chronicle*?"

Jackie nodded. "She's covering City Hall."

"Right," said McGowan. "But before that she was on the police beat for a month or so. Don't you remember, Jackie? She covered the murder of Mel Sweeten."

Jackie felt a rush of relief, which to Sarah Cook was just as obvious as her initial embarrassment had been. Of course! Marcella knew all about Jackie and McGowan's friendship through legitimate channels—her coverage of the Sweeten case. Jackie should never have doubted her friend's discretion.

Sarah, plainly amused by her friend's emotional turmoil, gave Jackie an innocent look. Jackie frowned at her, trying to look stern. "I'd better call Marcella this morning. Is everything all right?"

"Apparently so. The theft was interrupted, and not much was taken—just a couple of electronic things. Nothing irreplaceable. Lucky for your friend she's got a nosy old lady for a downstairs neighbor. The lady heard noises upstairs, and knew Marcella was working. So she went up and knocked on the door, and the guy went out a window."

"Glad to hear that, anyway."

From this point, the conversation became more general, as they discussed crime in Palmer. The boys took themselves off to the back of the bakery, where Emil Klinglehoffer had thoughtfully installed, about forty years ago, a pinball machine of the first order. The adults drank another cup of coffee, and Jackie reflected, as the little party broke up, that McGowan had added a great deal to the morning's pleasure. Now he would go off and do whatever it was he did with himself on Saturdays, when he wasn't working on a homicide case. Suddenly Jackie wanted to know what that would be. A trip to the hardware store? The grocery store? A tennis match?

She felt, for the first time since she had met McGowan, a pang of deep curiosity. She would really like to know more about this man. He was a very good friend for Peter.

CHAPTER 3

"Oh, poor you," Jackie sympathized. The two old friends were seated in Jackie's kitchen, where they had enjoyed a quiet supper of homemade cucumber soup, brown bread, and salad. Peter had gone to Isaac's house for the night; Jackie, thrilled to have an evening to call her own, had instantly telephoned Marcella Jacobs and invited her to supper, to commiserate with her friend about the burglary and to make certain, absolutely certain, that Marcella had been discreet with Michael McGowan. "What a rotten day it must have been."

"I'll say," Marcella agreed with a sigh. She shook back her long red-gold hair and grimaced. "First I lose my story, and then my apartment gets robbed. A double whammy."

"They didn't take much, though. Michael told me your neighbor interrupted them. That's lucky."

"Yeah, good old Mrs. Pancoast. A blessing and a curse." Marcella said this with a smile, and Jackie understood at once. She had suffered some very well-intentioned neighbors during her years in Kingswood.

"But it's not the stuff, so much, that I mind," Marcella went on.

"I know what you mean—it's the feeling."

"Right. Horrible. Somebody was poking around in my apartment. Creepy."

"What did he take? Stereo, that kind of thing, right?"

"Right." Marcella nodded. "Just the kind of thing that's hard to buy. Takes you a year to make up your mind, and the brands change all the time, and the technology. Enough to make you really insecure."

"I'll say," Jackie agreed. Her house was fairly free of gadgets—just an ancient but excellent stereo system, a tape player, and an old television. No CD player or microwave; she didn't even have remote control for the TV. Jackie's old-fashioned approach to technology perhaps betrayed a shyness in the presence of modern machines. Marcella was only slightly more up-to-date about such things. "What did the police think? Any chance you can get the things back?"

"Doubtful." Marcella shook her head; then a bright smile lit up her face. "Your lieutenant is really *cute,* Jackie!"

"He's not *mine,*" Jackie protested thinly with a wave of her hand.

Marcella gave her a look. "If I were you, I'd be very careful about saying things like that. People might think you meant it—and then where would you be?" Marcella gave her friend a shrewd look. "You'd better stop making pronouncements that you don't want to have to live with."

Marcella was making a good point. If Jackie went around saying she had no claims on Michael McGowan, people might take her seriously, and stake out their *own* claims. Jackie didn't include Marcella in her mental image of the cowgirls out to rope McGowan. As a rule, Marcella's tastes ran more to professors, tycoons, and holders of public office. Once, Marcella had nearly married the head of a famous museum in Washington. But still, you never knew.

"Point taken," said Jackie. "Well? Are the police going to get the things back?"

"No. I don't really care about the stereo equipment. The only thing I mind losing is my laptop."

"A computer?"

"Yeah. A good one. Old, reliable. You know. The kind of thing you really want to have forever."

"Can't you buy a new one? I'm sure the insurance would pay for it."

"Yeah, it'll cover it—but you know how things can be. I really liked working on that machine. The next one I get, who knows, might not be as good. Naturally my model is by now totally out-of-date. Heck, it's been around at least two years, so it's an antique."

"Right," agreed Jackie with a small laugh. "What did the police say?"

"Not much. They think it wasn't a very professional job, I guess. Just my luck to be ripped off by an amateur."

"Hmmm." Jackie thought it all over for a moment. "You know, I gave up believing in coincidences a while ago."

"What do you mean?"

"I mean that your computer at work was ripped off, and your computer at home." She gave her friend an inquiring glance. "What's the big secret story?"

Marcella frowned. "Nice try—but there's nothing too exciting inside my computers. Just a profile of our next mayor, Morton Slake."

"Oh." Jackie was disappointed. But, politics was politics. The press certainly had the power to put spokes in the wheel of any aspiring politician. "An impartial profile?"

"Well—of course." Marcella looked offended. "But I know what you mean. No, it's not necessarily a flattering one."

"Something that could sink his chances for winning the mayoral election?"

Marcella shrugged. "Doubtful. I mean, he isn't exactly a Boy Scout, but then who is? There are things that will make the race a little spicier, but nothing to sink his little ship. No real scandal." She reached absentmindedly for one of Jackie's home-baked ginger cookies. "Not really."

Jackie had a strong impression that Marcella wasn't leveling with her entirely. "You mean that?"

"Yes—I do." Marcella gave her friend an appraising glance. "For now."

"I see." Jackie knew better than to press Marcella for details. She would divulge the rest of it when the right moment arrived.

"So the Slake story was the only thing that was tampered with. At the paper, I mean."

"Right. Well, it's the only thing that was still in the system, right now. Everything else from last week had been filed already. I write a new 'Around Town' column for every Tuesday and Friday; they get filed on Monday and Thursday mornings. My computer files have a bunch of records, of course—notes, names, and addresses—but no actual stories, except that profile of Slake. Everything else is totally perishable—the city news gets written, read, and recycled all in the blink of an eye."

"I guess so," said Jackie, who had never thought about a reporter's work in those terms. Marcella was right— her stories were read and tossed out all in a single day. Jackie wasn't sure she'd like everyone throwing away all her hard work.

"I think someone's just out to get me. Professionally. To play a nasty practical joke." Marcella's voice was calm, as though she were accustomed to this type of thing. Jackie knew she'd had a problem, a severe problem, with a fellow reporter in Philadelphia. It was one of the reasons that Marcella had come back to Palmer—to get away from the ruinous rivalry of Jack Garfield.

"Like who?"

Marcella shrugged. "Anybody. There are about thirty-five other reporters who'd like to have my job. Most of them consider me an outsider, you know. Because I spent so long away from Palmer."

"They're probably just jealous," remarked Jackie thoughtfully. "Is there anybody who might have watched you while you made up a password for the story?"

Marcella shook her head. "Nobody but Bingo. And I trust him."

"Who's Bingo?"

"Oh, he's just another reporter." She briefly explained Stuart Allen's habit of giving his files random access codes. "He's always forgetting his passwords, and it's sort of a joke. But I talked to our head technician yesterday morning. He developed a safeguard for Bingo. A way to get around the password—so Bingo wouldn't constantly be pestering him."

"And I take it it works."

"Yeah. Matt showed it to me yesterday. No luck—there's nothing left where the story ought to be. But one of the utilities programs shows that the story used to be there."

"Hmmm." Jackie thought about it.

"You know, it doesn't really make a difference to me about the story. I still have my notes."

"Oh." Jackie looked at her friend. "Where?"

"At home."

Jackie and Marcella seemed to have the same thought at once. Marcella opened her eyes wide. "That is, I *think* they're at home."

"You didn't check for them?"

"No." She shook her head. "I was on my way to get them, yesterday afternoon—that's why I went home after the press conference. But of course I had to spend about four hours down at the precinct house, getting everything sorted out and reported. And I had dinner plans for last night—so I figured the Slake notes could wait till Monday."

"Let's go." Jackie rose suddenly and reached for a light jacket hanging on a peg by the back door. She opened the door to the backyard and whistled for Jake, who entered, sedate but curious. In the way of most dogs, he could always sense when an excursion was under way. Now, with one look at Jackie, he began to wag his tail in contented expectation. Marcella grabbed her jacket, and the two women departed, with Jake on his leash leading the way.

It was a short walk to Marcella's apartment on Cider Street, just across the Rodgers campus from where Jackie and Peter lived. The two women hurried silently down the lighted central walk of the campus, both preoccupied. When they arrived at Marcella's place, they proceeded up the stairs cautiously, quietly, as though yesterday's burglar might somehow still be on the premises. Marcella, as she turned her key in the lock, gave Jake an appreciative glance.

The apartment was in darkness; Marcella hastily flipped a switch near the door. Light flooded the small foyer and the living room, off to the right. Marcella led the way through the living room to a tiny office at the back. Here, sliding doors opened to reveal a closet with built-in drawers and cabinets. Marcella opened the second drawer from the top and groped with her right hand.

There was a moment's pause before she looked at Jackie.

"Now, what on earth has happened to my notebook?"

"At a guess," posited Jackie, "I'd say our thief has it." She looked at her friend sternly. "Marcella," she said in an authoritative voice, "I think you'd better tell me what's up. What have you got on Morton Slake?"

CHAPTER 4

On Monday morning Jackie Walsh knocked at the office door of her colleague, Fred Jackson, the cinematography instructor at Rodgers University. Jackson, a bearded bon vivant who had been teaching at Rodgers for thirty years, was one of those demigods that every campus seems to have—beloved by students and well regarded by his fellow faculty members, he was often seen striding along the campus walks, at the center of a group of six or seven students, all of them eagerly peppering him with questions.

In her undergraduate days, Jackie had been in awe of Fred—naturally. His opinion could make or break you in the film department, and for all of his bonhomie he was a stern judge of talent and dedication. Now that she and Fred were colleagues, Jackie admired his energy, and the stamina with which he greeted successive waves of enthusiastic students. He was a terrific teacher, no doubt about it. Jackie valued her privacy far too much to cultivate close friendships with her students; Fred, on the other hand, seemed always to be having lunch with undergraduates, watching films with them, giving them extra help on their papers, and in general behaving like a benevolent uncle toward the entire student body. It was a wonder he hadn't exhausted himself years ago.

Jackson was currently working on a summer-school project with some of the incoming seniors in the department. It was a documentary; they were deeply enmeshed in recording the workings of the local municipal government—tracing a bill through the city council, on its tortuous course through the channels of policy and politics.

Jackie, intrigued by Marcella's adventures, had been inspired on Sunday morning by the recollection of Fred's project. The council was voting tomorrow, and the last session of debate was scheduled for this afternoon. The television news would cover the session briefly, and Fred's seniors would be there. It was the perfect opportunity to find out more about Morton Slake.

Jackie felt she had a perfect excuse—ignorance of modern equipment. These days, the technical side of filmmaking was a mystery to Jackie, whose strength was a general knowledge of film history. In the fifteen years since her student days, videotape had replaced film, and with this change had come a whole new set of rules and expectations for the student filmmaker. Jackie was sure Fred and his students would welcome her. Now, seated in a comfortable armchair in Fred Jackson's office, she gave the cinematographer a shy smile.

"I'd like to tag along with your seniors today, if I may."

"No problem," replied Jackson agreeably. "Mind telling me what's up?"

"Oh, nothing. But I've got my lecture notes in order and I have a lot of free time. Besides, I've always wanted to learn more about videotape."

Jackson raised a bushy eyebrow. "You have?" He looked skeptical.

"Of course. I've only ever had hands-on experience with film. Well, you know, Fred—I'm not an artist or a technician; I'm a film historian. I'm weak on the technical side. I want to make up for that."

Jackson smiled and rubbed the tip of his nose with a large forefinger. "As I recall, Jackie, you really put your heart and soul into your senior film."

"I had to." Jackie laughed. "My heart and soul were all I had—no talent to speak of."

"Well, I wouldn't go *that* far," responded Jackson with his customary candor. "Anyway, you are of course welcome to tag along. You don't even need to ask. And, to demonstrate my confidence in you as a colleague, I'm not even going to ask you what the hell you're up to."

"Umm—"

"Because it's clear you're up to something. Not a doubt in the world." He waved a hand through the air. "But I respect your privacy and your right to any kind of cockamamie scheming you'd like. Don't give it a thought. Just don't get Uncle Fred in trouble with the mayor's office, all right?" He grinned and dismissed her with another wave, turning to a stack of papers that needed correcting.

Jackie, full of guilty knowledge, stole quietly out of Jackson's office. She hoped that she didn't get him and his seniors in trouble with the mayor. But, after all, Morton Slake was not the mayor, yet.

Jackie returned to her own small office, which was more of an airless cubbyhole than an office in the real sense. She sighed. Last fall, when the department chairman had been murdered, there had been some significant changing around of office space. Unfortunately, Jackie was in permanently bad odor with the department secretary, whose word about office space was law. She would probably always be stuck in this corner cubbyhole, no matter how much seniority she accumulated. It didn't matter—Jackie could think just as well here as in more posh quarters.

She sat down and thought now. She was quite proud of her plan. There wasn't even anything devious about it—which was lucky, because in the face of Marcella's reluctance to spill the beans on Slake, Jackie didn't want to slink around. This way was perfect—there could be nothing suspicious in the fact that she was tagging along on one of Fred Jackson's well-known projects. She could have a good long look at Morton Slake, and draw her own conclusions.

Jackie turned her thoughts once more to the events of Saturday evening. After she and Marcella had discovered the theft of the notebooks and tapes, Marcella had grown more silent than ever on the subject of Morton Slake. To Jackie's mind, there was only one answer. Marcella obviously must have acquired knowledge that would damage Slake. What other explanation could there be?

And the only person who would benefit from keeping that knowledge from being publicized was Morton Slake himself. Jackie had the feeling that Marcella was onto something, or that she was hoping to dig up something really big. But it seemed an extreme proof of her professional dedication not to denounce the theft.

When Jackie had challenged her, Marcella had put on her blandest look. "I don't know what you mean," she insisted. "There's nothing special to the story, really. It's just one of those 'Here He Is' stories. Morton Slake, Citizen and Leader."

"Come off it."

"Honestly." Marcella had insisted, but the look in her eyes had given her away. Jackie knew there was something more, and that Marcella was stubbornly refusing to share it. But there was probably a good reason for it—such as that it was all, as yet, an unconfirmed hunch.

"You'll tell me the whole thing someday, won't you?" asked Jackie.

Marcella merely nodded, and with that Jackie had been

forced to be contented. What was worse, Marcella had extracted from Jackie a promise not to mention the stolen notebooks and tapes to anyone, including Michael McGowan. Jackie, with her fingers crossed behind her back, had promised. She had begun to feel that Marcella might be in some sort of personal danger; and that if she persisted in playing by her reporter's rules, she might get hurt. A promise not to be pushy and nosy could only be honored up to a point—beyond which, the duties of friendship took precedence.

Jackie had a copy of the outline the summer-school students had drawn up. The video would trace the course of a single piece of municipal legislature—a new gun-control law—through the protracted process of the local government. The video would show Palmer officials at work—the mayor in his office at City Hall, the police commissioner, the members of the city council, the head of the city budget commission, and the district attorney—handling the legislature as it came to them, giving opinions and orders, asking for research, and finally offering their backing or their opposition. With the cameras rolling, the politicians would no doubt be likely to put their best foot forward; it would be interesting to see how the vote came out in the city council. The mayor was known to be opposed to any form of gun control. But Morton Slake's mayoral campaign called him the "Friend of Law and Order." It would be interesting to see if he had the strength to break with the mayor on this issue—with the cameras recording the council debate, it would be difficult for Slake to come out against the bill. Of course, whatever happened before the cameras might have nothing to do with the discussions in closed session—nor with telephone calls and quiet lunches between the mayor and Slake. Jackie strongly doubted that the gun-control bill would pass. Not until Palmer had a new mayor.

She drew a yellow legal pad toward her and began to make notes. There seemed to be a lot of things that she ought to be on the lookout for in her trip downtown with Fred Jackson and his filmmakers.

Not far from the campus of Rodgers University, in the squat brick building that served as the headquarters for the local police precinct, Michael McGowan was in his office, with the door shut, talking in a very low voice to a curly-haired man of fifty or so who occupied the visitor's chair.

The visitor, whose bushy red-brown hair was fading to gray, was Cosmo Gordon, Palmer's chief medical examiner. Gordon moved a finger to his lips, a cautionary sign. Then he glanced casually at his wristwatch. "Let's go to the Juniper for a cheeseburger, Mike."

Gordon rose and pulled on an old weather-beaten raincoat. He adjusted his horn-rimmed glasses and gave McGowan a look. Reluctantly McGowan pulled on his own raincoat, straightened his necktie, and followed Gordon out through the noisy main offices of the University Precinct.

A four-block walk through the intermittent rain and gusty winds brought them to the Juniper Tavern, a comfortable local bar and eatery. A favorite place of both the university crowd and the locals, the Juniper was a kind of melting pot, halfway between the two worlds of town and gown. McGowan and Gordon favored it because it wasn't popular with their colleagues from the force. It was a place, therefore, where the young detective and the medical examiner could freely discuss their cases, without fear of being overheard and misinterpreted. A safe haven. What was more, the food was perfect—homemade soups, fresh salads, juicy burgers, and frosty beers. What more could anyone want?

Neither man spoke until they were settled in their customary place, the last wooden booth in the back, and had given their lunch orders to Rachel Gibson, waitress par excellence. Rachel was friendly, prompt, cheerful, and discreet—virtues that had netted her a small fortune in tips over the years. She had worked hard to cultivate her favored position among the campus bigwigs who hobnobbed here, the occasional politicians, and of course Cosmo Gordon, who had been using the Juniper for his off-the-record consultations for decades.

Rachel had been working at the Juniper for almost as long as Gordon had been coming here for lunch—twenty-two years. In the old days, when Gordon had been a young forensic specialist on the rise, he had lunched here with a wide variety of colleagues. His most frequent lunchtime companion in those days had been Matt Dugan—a large, cheery, beer-bellied beat cop who had, it later emerged, been on the take. He had been dismissed from the Palmer force, but for six or seven years after his dismissal, Gordon had continued to have lunch with him regularly. Gradually, however, Dugan had faded from the scene.

The first few times that Gordon and Dugan had turned up at the Juniper after Dugan's dismissal, Rachel almost hadn't recognized the former policeman. He had looked so strangely different out of uniform.

Today, although Rachel Gibson had no way of knowing it, it was Dugan who was on Gordon's mind. To Gordon, the setting seemed right. He and Matt had been friends for many years—more like brothers, really—and much of their time had been spent here. Those had been the happy days, golden days for Matt, before his troubles set in.

Unlike most of the force, Cosmo Gordon hadn't deserted Matt when his problems began. Gordon didn't give a damn about the idea of guilt by association, and as M.E. he was freer to do what he chose than many of the cops on the force. But Gordon's attentions to Dugan had been in vain. The original affliction had been gambling, but Dugan's troubles began to follow a well-worn path. Predictably, he had soon fallen into debt, owing large amounts to some of Palmer's big boys. Worried for his safety, he borrowed where he could.

The loans hadn't helped—they had merely exacerbated the debts, made them deeper and more insurmountable. Drink had relieved the anxiety, at first—or thus Dugan had believed.

Finally there had seemed no alternative but to help himself to some of the ready money that was offered freely, for any cop who needed to bring home a little extra, and who didn't care much about the source. Gordon imagined that to Dugan it must have seemed the only alternative.

Over five swift years, the loan sharks and the mob boys had drained the pride and the life from Matt Dugan, third-generation Palmer cop, former Palmer Police Rookie of the Year, honorary treasurer of the Policemen's Benevolent League, head of the Youth Charity Projects. As far as Cosmo Gordon was concerned, Dugan's murder, last November, in the seedy alley behind Leanna's Piano Parlor, had more or less been just a formality. Matt Dugan had died long ago.

In the nine months since Dugan's death, very little progress had been made on the case. Gordon was disturbed. But today he had sensed a chink, a crack. At long last, progress.

"The gun, Mikey," Gordon said as their beers arrived. "I think it's been found."

McGowan took a long look at Gordon. There wasn't any need to ask which gun. For nine months, the two friends had agreed on this telegraphic way of communicating facts about the Dugan case. Each of them had his reasons.

Nine months ago, Evan Stillman, recently promoted from lieutenant to captain, had assigned two detectives on the homicide squad to the case. (When Gordon challenged the assignment as cheap, Stillman ignored him. It was, as he pointed out, a lot more attention than most derelicts got from the police.) But the Palmer police still had no idea who had pulled the trigger on Dugan.

"Where?"

"I've just been looking through the report on a drive-by shooting in West Palmer. The weapon was recovered from the drainage ditch behind the old steelworks. I think we've got it, Mike."

To McGowan, it had sometimes seemed over the last few months that Gordon had become obsessed with finding Dugan's killer. At first, McGowan had been interested—especially when Gordon had told him that Dugan had uncovered some kind of corruption scandal in the city government. Gordon had been persuaded that Dugan had been killed to silence him.

Now, nine months later with no trace of a lead, the young lieutenant was more inclined to believe that they would never find the killer. There were plenty of other, more pressing matters before the Palmer police, anyway, and they had spent a lot of time tracking down false leads, especially about the gun. But maybe, at last, something decent had turned up.

"A match?"

"I think so. I need your help to confirm it, though."

"We'll send it up to the lab," suggested McGowan halfheartedly.

Gordon gave him a skeptical look, which McGowan understood. There was a good chance that there might be room for error on this. It smelled corrupt.

"All right, not the lab," agreed McGowan. "But how can we get confirmation?"

"We can hire a private expert to give us an opinion."

"I suppose so. But won't that look kind of strange coming from the police?"

"Absolutely. That's why I need your help. We have to think of a likely outsider who is curious enough about the crime to want some information, but whom we can trust. Absolutely. Somebody who can go get answers to our questions for us."

McGowan took a long pull at his beer, put down his mug, and sighed. "All right. I'll ask her."

"I knew you would." Gordon smiled and bit into his cheeseburger.

CHAPTER 5

The chambers of the Palmer city council, which occupied the entire second floor of the Municipal Building, were old-fashioned, respectable, and rather grand. The large limestone building, an excellent example of the Classical Revival, was a little over a century old. It was the product of an age that had glorified public office, rather than public officials; some of this ambience still lingered.

Jackie had paid many visits here over the years, the way most people did in their lifetimes. She had come in frustration to the department of motor vehicles, housed on the ground floor; twice, on an errand for her mother, she had been to the property tax office, down the hall from motor vehicles. Once, Jackie had visited the marriage license bureau, way back when—its entrance was around the back, presumably to provide a decent degree of separation between the matrimonial hopefuls and the angry motorists paying their parking fines.

Never before, however, had Jackie penetrated past the elaborate security desks and metal detectors to the upper air of the city government offices. Now, meekly retrieving her handbag and clipping on a VISITOR tag, she made her way up the grand old circular staircase, with its brass banister, to the second floor. Here were the offices of

Palmer's mayor, high-ranking city officials, and council members.

Soon Jackie was quietly tucked in among the busy half dozen or so of Fred Jackson's film students in the chamber of the city council, a vast, high-ceilinged expanse at whose center was a magnificent mahogany table, one that could easily seat thirty. The film students had taken up a position just inside and to the right of the large double doors that led into the council chamber. Across the room from Fred's seniors were three news teams from the local networks. Today's debate would be televised, if anybody at the station office found it interesting enough.

That was the problem with the issues confronting local government, Jackie reflected. The interest never seemed to match the importance of the topic, and the process of the city legislature couldn't possibly compete for airtime with halfway scandalous, pseudodocumentary programs— *Dangerous True Rescue!* or *Your Right to Know, With Jerry Waters.* Small wonder that the media always felt compelled to dig for dirt, she thought. They were obliged to entertain so they could pull in the ratings.

Jackie shook her mind free from such depressing deliberations and walked toward the other end of the room. There, an enormous window with wood paneling and floor-to-ceiling mullioned glass looked out over Monument Park, a small green spot in the busy heart of downtown. Jackie looked down at the dogwoods and azaleas in bloom, pink and white and pale purple in the spring sunlight.

The city council members were taking their seats, talking quietly to one another, their expressions giving clear evidence that, to a one, they were conscious of the presence of the cameras. The men wore gray suits and buttercup-yellow "power ties"; the women had on red dresses à la Nancy Reagan. On almost everyone's face Jackie saw the

look that people get when they are trying not to mug for
a camera. She reflected that televising the council votes
would probably ensure the vapidity of the discussion ahead.
Luckily, she didn't plan to stick around for the whole of
it.

She looked away from the preening council members,
whose insecurity before the huge-eyed cameras was a pain-
ful thing to behold. Through enormous sliding oak doors
she could see into an adjoining conference room, hung
with large oils depicting important moments of Palmer civic
history. There was Eugene Ward Palmer, the city founder,
in breeches and a red waistcoat, holding up the land patent
granted him by George II. Next to his portrait was a battle
scene from the War of 1812, in which Palmer's local militia
had played a tiny but heroic part. At the far end of the room
was a late nineteenth-century portrait of Matthew Newcomer, the city's most famous mayor. Newcomer had been
a handsome, scholarly, wealthy gentleman, much given to
philanthropy. He had been one of those rare civic leaders
who can move among the people without losing a shred of
their dignity.

All in all, Jackie thought, as she returned her gaze to
the waiting council members, the atmosphere here had a
way of making modern politics and modern politicians
seem shabby and shallow. She wondered that the council
members didn't feel like impostors, sitting here day after
day. But probably these people were no worse, morally and
intellectually, than most of their predecessors.

The film students, serious and technical, were moving
about taking light readings, testing sound levels, and plug-
ging in masses of tangled-looking wires. There were four
young men, in jeans with button-down shirts, and all sport-
ing the ponytail that now seemed obligatory for every male
undergraduate, not merely the fine arts and architecture

students. The three young women wore black—black skirts, black blouses, black stockings, and black shoes. They had very short hair, which they brushed out of their eyes with businesslike efficiency. Despite the uniform, they all looked remarkably individual.

Across the room were the paid professionals, making jokes and looking slightly bored, with their massive array of equipment, all of it looking hard and out of place in the finely proportioned council chamber. Jackie recognized one of the lesser lights from Channel 6, a sharp-nosed man of thirty-five or so who always wore a trench coat on camera. He was not wearing one now, she noted. Would he put it on to sum up the city council meeting?

At a minute before one, Morton Slake appeared and took his seat at the head of the table. He looked well groomed and calm as he nodded briskly to the other council members. He leaned over and spoke to the woman at his right, making some sort of joke. They both laughed, and Slake, with an easy, practiced movement, reached out and flipped on a small microphone on the table before him.

Jackie watched as a tall, blond, puffy-lipped young man took up a firm position behind Slake, folding his hands before him and glancing restlessly around the room. The motion of his flickering eyes reminded Jackie of Secret Service agents, at least as they were represented in the movies. This boy with the puffy lips was probably Slake's bodyguard, she thought—although he didn't look particularly tough. And there was really no reason for Slake to have a bodyguard. Or was there? Or maybe Slake thought a person in his position needed an escort, the way some people thought they needed cellular phones.

The puffy-lipped young man whispered into Slake's ear; the council president looked up and nodded toward Fred

Jackson, catching his eye. Jackie admired the smooth greeting—which by its very inessentiality could not fail to ingratiate. Morton Slake was a man who knew his way around the political world.

Now, in a cultured, deep voice, Slake called the meeting to order. The secretary was called upon to read out the minutes of the last meeting, which had included a rather dull debate on the issue of afternoon garbage collection. Fred Jackson's students began to concentrate earnestly on their task, whispering urgently to one another, looking serious.

For five minutes Jackie watched Morton Slake intently. He was certainly at ease in the limelight—there was not, in his manner, even the slightest hint of self-consciousness at the cameras. The discussion progressed from last week's meeting to the issue of unused paid vacation for city clerks. Jackie, seeing that everyone was momentarily absorbed, backed quietly out of the council chamber into the hallway.

If Morton Slake, or his puffy-lipped young aide, noticed her departure, Jackie was unaware.

In the city council chamber, all was going smoothly for Fred Jackson's students. The council members had been cooperative and kind, and the young filmmakers were well on their way to documenting an historic occasion. The meeting began to shift quickly from garbage to guns, and with mounting excitement those present in the room realized that Morton Slake, in an unprecedented break with the mayor's expressed point of view, was speaking in favor of the gun-control law.

That Slake and the mayor might part company—especially on such a politically explosive issue—was an unexpected turn of events, and the reporters in the room had been visibly enlivened by the idea. The council members, too, were apparently caught unawares. As Slake wound up his speech in favor of stricter control of handguns, the reporters scrambled for interview positions. Most of them knew that this was their only chance at the big story—by tomorrow, they would have been shouldered out of the way by others with more seniority or on-camera value. Today, however, the poor drudges who had been sent to cover garbage collection were having their moment.

Fred Jackson looked around for Jackie Walsh, who was missing out on all the excitement. For the third or fourth time, he wondered what she was up to. Jackson knew as well as anyone that Jackie had no more than a passing interest in the techniques of shooting videotape. She already knew more about documentary techniques than anyone in the department, except for Fred himself. Clearly, she had tagged along for reasons of her own.

To Jackie's right there was a long corridor, with offices along both sides. At the far end was a single wooden door with a frosted-glass panel—the kind of door that had led to the office of Jackie's dentist, when she was a little girl. The kind of door that Sam Spade's office had in *The Maltese Falcon*. Jackie could see gold lettering on the panel: "City Council President" and below that, in a brighter, evidently newer gold, "Morton K. Slake."

As she stood watching, a robust, gray-haired woman in a businesslike blue suit came briskly out of the door. She held a two-inch-thick sheaf of papers in one hand, and there was an expression of mild annoyance on her competent-looking face. Jackie decided that the harassed air was probably a permanent part of the woman's countenance, like her large horn-rimmed bifocals and the thick waves of gray hair, which looked as fixed as cement. She stopped briefly before an open door at the right of Slake's office.

"Maureen, I have to go upstairs to the photocopier. Want anything?"

Jackie couldn't make out the reply. The stout woman nodded and rushed past Jackie, stirring up a small breeze as she went.

Jackie was willing to bet that the brusque, blue-suited woman was Slake's private secretary. She glimpsed quickly toward the second door, marked "City Council Administrative Staff." Within was a hive of aides, assistants, and other gofer types common in busy political offices. An efficient-looking blonde near the door, with a tiny microphone suspended before her mouth, manipulated the buttons on the switchboard before her with long, red-nailed fingers. "Morton Slake's office, Jennifer speaking. How may we help you?"

Well, well, thought Jackie.

Secretary gone and receptionist in another room. The open door before her beckoned. After all, it wouldn't hurt to just poke her head in. Get a feeling for the man.

For a split second, Jackie wondered if she was losing her grip. She had joined Fred Jackson's excursion under false pretenses, and here she was about to spy on the city council president's office, with no reasonable excuse at her fingertips. It wasn't as though the man's dirty linen would be hanging out here, for all the world to see.

On the other hand, it couldn't hurt to look around. Jackie was willing to admit that her friend Marcella's dilemma had piqued her curiosity. And now that she was *here*—well, she really ought to take advantage. With her connections on the police force and her experience in the ways of sleuthing, Jackie felt she could definitely be of service to Marcella, if she only knew what Marcella was up to. Besides, Marcella had come to her for help. Well, more or less.

Judging by the thick sheaf of papers that the secretary had taken with her upstairs, Jackie might easily have five minutes to herself if she dared to poke her head in and look around. Jackie imagined that Slake kept the gray-haired woman hopping whenever he was in his office. He looked like the kind of "busy executive" who wouldn't deign to sharpen his own pencil. The woman, if she had any sense, would probably take advantage of his absence at the council meeting to have a cup of coffee somewhere, or to run an important errand, or to speak to her colleagues on the mayoral staff.

Jackie took a deep breath and went on in, past the secretary's vacant post, through another door, and into Morton Slake's private office.

CHAPTER 6

Within Morton Slake's well-made and well-furnished office, a deep quiet reigned. Jackie, tiptoeing across a thick Persian rug, paused before a shelf full of photographs that displayed the predictable stages in the career of a real-estate developer and city politician. She beheld a very young Morton Slake breaking ground for a shopping center; Morton Slake shaking hands with a local ice-hockey star; Morton Slake and Mrs. Slake opening the new pedestrian mall. That was the commercial life—the next group of photos were more civic-minded. Morton Slake on Founder's Day with the mayor; Morton Slake and the police commissioner at the opening of the new city prison; Morton Slake in a city park with a troop of Boy Scouts; Morton Slake in a shelter for homeless women.

Jackie turned away from the photographs to take in a huge blowup of an aerial view of the heart of downtown Palmer. The black-and-white photo claimed half of the far wall; on it, all of Slake's important real-estate holdings were outlined in vivid pinks and blues; from this distance, it looked as though he owned a great proportion of the city. Which, of course, he did.

The idea of a real-estate mogul as mayor disconcerted

Jackie, who had rather old-fashioned ideas about impartiality and civic responsibility. She supposed, however, that he could do just as much damage in his present post on the city council. In a way, as mayor he would be more open to scrutiny.

She turned to look at a row of books standing on a small credenza against another wall. There was nothing much worth looking at—a lavish photo book about skyscrapers, four hardcover soldier-of-fortune-style thrillers, a thesaurus, and two books by Donald Trump. There were no surprises here, either, Jackie reflected.

From somewhere behind the large mahogany desk came the sound of a cricket chirping. The sound repeated itself three times, as Jacke grew dimly aware that it came from a small telephone on the window ledge behind Slake's desk. Without giving herself time to consider the possibilities, she took three steps toward the window and picked up the phone.

"Morton Slake's office." Jackie made her voice as coolly professional as possible.

"Margaret, thank God you picked up. It's Bambi," said a woman's voice. From the degree of background noise in the transmission, Jackie concluded that Bambi, whoever she might be, was calling from a moving car. "Listen, I hate to ask you, but could you just tell him that I can't make lunch? Don't let him growl at you. Tell him I'll call later."

"All right," said Jackie, doing her best to sound busy and preoccupied. Now she would have to leave a message. But it was going to be tricky. Maybe leave it on Margaret's desk, signed "an anonymous friend"?

"Thanks, Margaret. I knew you would. I don't think he appreciates you the way he should," said Bambi, gushing. Her voice made Jackie think of someone long-legged, blond, and not particularly smart; someone shrewd and rather unfeeling, who had nothing much to do except to shop or visit her hairdresser, after the aerobics and the three-times-weekly tennis match. Jackie was filled with an instantaneous loathing, a deep mingling of envy, insecurity, contempt, and pity. It was a feeling Jackie hadn't known since Mary Lee Boddicker had stolen her boyfriend, and ruined her life, in the eighth grade.

Bambi was prattling on. "You're a doll. He means it when he says he'll look after you. Ciao, darling!"

Bambi, whoever she might be, rang off in a haze of background transmission noise. Jackie quietly rested the telephone back on its ledge and furrowed her brow in thought.

"A call for you?" said a voice behind her.

Jackie gulped and whirled. Standing in the doorway was a tall, lean man of forty or so, in a well-cut dark blue suit and a somewhat playful striped shirt. He had a generous mouth, and his slate-blue eyes looked at Jackie with a mixture of curiosity and amusement. He seemed familiar to her, but in her momentary mortified confusion, as she inched away from Morton Slake's private telephone line, it was impossible for Jackie to place him.

"Um—" Never had she felt quite so inadequate.

The tall man crossed his arms and rubbed his chin thoughtfully, gazing at Jackie carefully. He appeared to be sizing her up. Probably trying to decide whether or not to arrest her, thought Jackie, with a sinking feeling in her stomach.

"Um—" she said once more.

A faint smile seemed to flicker on the man's lips. "Or maybe you were just lost?" Evidently he had decided to give Jackie a graceful way out. "And you answered the phone, just trying to be helpful. Yes?"

"Yes." Jackie had found her voice. "Yes, I was, actually. I mean, I came in here, and then the phone rang and I thought the least I could do was take a message—"

The man glanced at the telephone. Even to Jackie it had been obvious that she had answered the man's private line. An official-looking telephone, with an array of a hundred buttons and lights, was perched majestically on the mahogany desk. Of course, since Slake was in the council meeting, and Margaret the secretary had gone upstairs, the receptionist would hold Slake's calls. The only reason for answering the other line would be to find out who was calling on it. It seemed embarrassingly obvious to Jackie now—but she had never dreamed she'd be caught in the act!

Morton Slake's visitor was still regarding her carefully. "That was Bambi, yes?"

"Um—"

"Here." The man reached over and tore the top sheet off a message cube. "I bet she can't make lunch. Am I right?"

"Um—"

He scrawled a hasty message and left it on Slake's chair. "Come on, then. Let's get you out of here before you get yourself in some kind of trouble."

He gestured Jackie out of the inner sanctum, out through Margaret's office, and into the safety of the long corridor. When they had gone a few steps from the entrance to Slake's office, the man grabbed Jackie by the elbow and pulled her into a shallow-crescent-shaped recess in the wall. He smiled and stuck out a hand.

"Nate Northcote," he said.

"I'm Jackie Walsh," replied Jackie, her voice still with a hint of a quaver in it. She knew now why the man seemed familiar. He was the city's prosecuting attorney. She took his proffered hand and shook it, thinking that it would be smart to make friends. Under the circumstances. Then she could just sneak quietly back into the council chamber, where she belonged, and forget this embarrassing interlude.

Nate Northcote held her hand in his a moment longer than was strictly necessary, and smiled down at her from his great height. "Pleased to meet you, Jackie Walsh. Suppose you let me buy you lunch, and you can tell me all about what you were doing in Slake's office."

"Um—"

"That is, unless you'd rather wait here for Margaret, and tell her instead."

Jackie glanced quickly at her watch and cleared her throat nervously. "Thank you very much, but I don't have time for lunch. I have a— I have to be somewhere in fifteen minutes."

Northcote frowned good-naturedly. "Well, then, it will have to be dinner. If you're free tonight, it would be my very great pleasure. And don't say 'Um—' "

The monosyllable died on Jackie's lips, and she smiled. She was finding her confidence again. "How about a cup of coffee in the faculty cafeteria at Rodgers?" she responded, rather proud of this solution. "Five o'clock."

"God! College cafeteria coffee." His blue eyes twinkled. "That's no way to treat someone who's just saved your hide. Make it the Juniper Tavern, and you're on."

"All right," said Jackie, finding herself strangely willing to compromise. "The Juniper it is. At five."

"And then maybe we'll talk about dinner?"

"Coffee," said Jackie firmly, feeling that she had better be on her guard. It was only Monday. Heaven knew what Peter would think if she went out on a dinner date with some man on a Monday.

Jackie thought it would be rather nice to have dinner with Nate Northcote, Palmer's prosecuting attorney. But not on a Monday. It would be much better on a Friday, when she could relax.

"Whaddaya mean, you didn't take the message?" whined Morton Slake.

Margaret Leaming's stout cheeks flushed with irritation, and her heavy eyelids flickered. This was the third time that Slake had questioned her about Bambi's call. It was bad enough that she, Margaret Leaming, was expected to take a message from that little tramp. Not that she ever did. She never bothered to pick up Morton's private line. He only gave the number to his girlfriends. Margaret had principles.

Margaret Leaming didn't believe a married man should have girlfriends—and that went double for a married man in public life. It was just a sign of weakness, although Morton Slake and the others like him thought it was a sign of virility or power. But Margaret Leaming knew that eventually those pert little pigeons always came home to roost.

It was just dumb luck that Bambi—or rather the existence of Bambi—hadn't ruined Morton's chances for the election. If Marie Zug ever got wind of Bambi, it would be all over. With regard to Morton's girlfriend troubles, this was the only thing that worried Margaret Leaming, just at present. She didn't care about messages from Bambi, lunch with Bambi, Morton Slake's pathetic desire to keep Bambi around. He would soon move on to a new one.

Being a woman of sense, Margaret Leaming believed—
and had always believed—that Morton Slake was a wildly
self-indulgent, spoiled, shallow man. In her view, those
were the very characteristics that most counted for his
success. Those, and the fact that Margaret herself had
always been there, doing the work, pulling him out of
problems, keeping him in line, making sure the day's work
got done. Morton Slake was what the public saw; what they
didn't see was Margaret Leaming, behind everything that
Slake did.

By and large, Morton Slake was hugely ambitious, and
he didn't give a damn who he stepped on. The fact that
he had so few enemies in Palmer was entirely thanks to
Margaret's intervention. She was constantly pouring oil on
the waters, mending fences, and soothing bruised egos. She
was forever sending little presents to people whom Morton
had offended, or reminding him about birthdays, or making
sure that he didn't break important engagements in a fit of
temper. Even so, he was known to be hotheaded, and he
was not universally liked. The miracle was that he was
not universally despised. That was Margaret Leaming's
personal miracle, her own triumph. It wasn't a small thing,
not at all.

For twenty years, Margaret Leaming had groomed
Morton Slake and made him perfectly palatable to the
world at large. This she had done not because she
liked him, or cared for him in any way. She was old
enough to be his mother, but she had never wanted
to be anybody's mother. The thought was dreadful to
her.

No, she had cared for him and handled him and brought
him along because she was just as ambitious as he. And—
thanks to her intelligence, her competence, and her iron

will—she was far, far more successful, in her own way, than most people would ever be.

But Margaret Leaming was also a realist. Only in a few isolated moments in time were women permitted, by the world at large, to succeed in an open forum. Mostly, through the ages, women had been obliged—sometimes on pain of death—to hide their lights under a bushel. Margaret was good at being in charge without appearing to be in charge. Really, the only person who knew how much she did for Morton Slake was Morton Slake. And God knew he would never tell.

Margaret didn't really care about fame. It was perfectly fine with her if the world was only dimly aware of her existence. She knew the truth; she had held in her hands the raw power of pure control. It was she who had built the Morton Slake real-estate empire—not with money, but with wits, with savvy, with an eye for the main chance. She had also run the city council for ten years. For the last year, she had been gearing up to be mayor, in her own way.

Unfortunately for Morton Slake, however, Margaret had in the last few weeks begun to suspect that she would not after all be mayor.

Not that Morton Slake was going to lose—as far as Margaret Leaming could tell, there wasn't a prayer of that. Jane Bellamy, the urban planning specialist from the university, had foolishly discussed the probability of raising taxes to pay for city services. Morton knew (because Margaret had taught him long ago) that people always, always vote with their wallets, and not with their heads.

Morton's platform called for greater law and order; was there a soul in Palmer, or in any twentieth-century city in America, who would not wish for greater law and order?

But, sensibly, Morton Slake had neatly avoided the question of how the city—struggling, like any city, to keep water mains from bursting and sanitation systems functioning and roads paved—would be able to afford such a luxury as "law and order."

Slake's budget made no provision for wage increases for the police department; nor had he provided the city, in his plan, with the additional prison space that would be so desperately needed if he achieved his stated goal— to put "every crook in Palmer behind bars." In fact, Morton Slake (or, rather, Morton and Margaret) proposed to cut city services across the board in order to save money. If he didn't do that, he would be obliged to raise taxes, and he would lose the election. His only stated position, in fact—despite the campaign ads about law and order—had been the sudden turnabout on the gun-control bill.

All in all, Margaret thought that was a bad misstep. Morton was making enemies again, and she hadn't been there in the council chamber to stop him. When she had voiced her worries to him, he had merely laughed. "The mayor's already given me his endorsement. What's he gonna do? Take it away because I spoke out against Saturday Night Specials?"

Margaret had been forced to concede the logic of it. Still, the sudden public break with the mayor's position made her uncomfortable. And she knew who was behind it.

Despite the blunder about the gun-control bill, however, Margaret Leaming thought Morton Slake—her protégé, her product, whom she had tended as carefully as any 4-H member tends his prize sow—was a shoo-in. His candidacy, like all of his professional life, had been carefully wrapped up and neatly packaged. It was unlikely that anybody would sniff out the pathetic truth about his budgetary vision, his minimal grasp of the important lessons of government, before election time. After that, it would be too late anyway, and Morton would win them over with the sheer force of his personality.

If, of course, he didn't blow it.

"Margaret, I don't get it. Bambi says she talked to you."

"Well, she's either lying or mistaken. Take your pick, Morton."

"How dare you?"

Margaret smiled thinly. "I dare whatever I please around here, as you very well know. Your little piece of trouble is either lying or mistaken."

"Well then, how do you account for this?" Pale with rage, Morton Slake held up a square of white paper. At the top, small, neat red print told the world that this was a "Message From Margaret Leaming." Below, in a small space provided, was written: "Bambi can't make lunch. Will call."

"Maybe your little lieutenant wrote it."

"I take it you mean Tim. No, Margaret. Admit that you slipped up, that you came down off your high horse and took the message."

Margaret Leaming stared at him. Sometimes Morton did this—went into a nitpicking rage about some tiny detail. At first these rages had frightened her, but over the years she had learned to ignore them. Sometimes she even found them amusing, but she was very careful not to show her amusement.

Slake's voice had taken on a curiously precise quality. He seemed to use the very alphabet differently when he was in one of his moods. Margaret listened, fascinated. "Bambi *says* she talked to you, Margaret. She dialed this office. A woman answered. My private line, not out there.

And here's the message." He waved it under her nose. "Admit it."

"For God's sake, Morton." Margaret peered at the message square. "After twenty years, can't you even tell? That's not my writing." She shook her head at him in pity. "That's not my writing at all."

CHAPTER 7

"Really nice," Jackie was saying. She leaned back in the chair at her kitchen table and stretched her legs out. On the floor at her feet, Jake shifted. Jackie stroked the fur on Jake's shoulders with her bare toes, and smiled across the table at her friend Marcella.

Jackie was relating the story of her adventures downtown. She glossed over certain aspects of being discovered by Nate Northcote in Morton Slake's office, allowing Marcella to conclude that they had met by chance at the council meeting. "Plus, he's funny, and good-looking. And tall."

"You're going to break Michael McGowan's heart," protested Marcella earnestly.

"Oh, don't be silly. Michael and I are just friends."

"Admit that you like having him be hopelessly in love with you."

"There's nothing hopeless about it."

"Aha!" Marcella pointed a sharp finger of accusation.

"No, I don't mean that either. Michael and I are just friends." She thought she probably spoke the truth. After all, if he was hopelessly in love, he had a funny way of showing it. He did call her—but only when he needed information about someone at Rodgers University, or a connection with

61

the university administration. Just this week, he had called to ask a favor relating to some case or other. And she had duly gone to the Hertz Laboratory in the graduate school of physics to request and to collect test results of some sort. "He said it was a sensitive case," said Jackie, "but he wouldn't tell me what it was about. Just didn't want to be seen asking for the information himself. And he didn't exactly follow up with a bouquet of yellow roses. Or even daisies. It doesn't take much to think of bringing someone daisies, let's face it." Jackie smiled ruefully. "There was a time, I admit it, when I thought he and I might hit it off. But it's been ages, and so far he hasn't even asked if he could hold my hand."

Marcella had listened to Jackie's tale with an air of sympathy and puzzlement.

"Funny," she said at last. "Because he sure seemed moonstruck to me when we talked about you the other day."

"Well, he's not. He likes me, that's all. And finds me a useful connection." Jackie's voice might have contained a slight edge of mystified resentment, if it hadn't been for the satisfaction, still warm in her memory, of her cup of coffee yesterday with Nate Northcote. He was, after all, much more her type, she told herself. They had only had time for a quick chat. Northcote had politely refrained from grilling her about her adventure in Slake's office, accepting her explanation that the meeting had bored her, and that she wanted to scope out locations for the rest of the students' documentary. For his part, Northcote had listened with an amused grin on his face, and then asked her to a cocktail party with him on Friday evening. A swanky affair at the house of Max Greenaway, the police commissioner.

"*That* should be interesting," commented Marcella. Greenaway was quite a figure in city life—eccentric, well connected, and extremely rich.

"I can't wait," said Jackie. "I've always wanted to meet him."

It was sort of funny, she remarked to Marcella, that she couldn't seem to get away from the law, but that was okay. Over the months of her friendship with Michael McGowan, Jackie had discovered in herself an unsuspected pleasure in forensics. Knowing Nate Northcote would at least provide her with a new angle on the criminal element in Palmer.

"Hmm," said Marcella, spreading a nice runny camembert on a cracker. "Well, anyhow, what I really want to know is what you think you were doing sneaking around in Morton Slake's office. I hope you didn't mention my name."

"Marcella." Jackie was disgusted. She reached for her glass of red wine and took a large swig. "How could you?"

"Okay, okay. Sorry." Marcella managed to look sheepish, brushing a lustrous red lock back from her forehead. "Of course you didn't mention my name. What *did* you do?"

"Oh, just snooped around. Tried to figure out what he was like. His secretary looked like a sturdy, competent type. So I guess we know who really does all the work of the city council president." Jackie raised her eyebrows.

"Ain't it always the way?" agreed Marcella lightly. "That's Margaret Leaming. She's been running Morton Slake since he was a tadpole."

"Aha."

"Right. She's efficient, businesslike, smart, and dedicated. We could do worse than have her for mayor in Palmer."

"You've got a point," Jackie replied. She helped herself to a cracker with cheese.

"But what about Slake? What did you think of him? You did see him at the meeting, didn't you?"

"Yeah. He's smooth, like silk."

"Tell me something I don't know. What else?"

"Oh, I don't know. His office doesn't tell you much, does it?"

"Nope," agreed Marcella.

"Except, I guess, that he reads books by Donald Trump."

Marcella chuckled. "Are you sure he reads them? Maybe he just keeps them on the shelf for show."

"An accurate point," retorted Jackie, pretending to stifle a yawn. "Good thing you're the reporter and I'm not, Little Miss Factual."

Marcella stuck her tongue out at Jackie, who ignored her and thought again about the books in Slake's office. "No, I have no idea if he reads them. But there they are on his shelf. Just what you'd expect from Morton Slake."

"Right."

"But what I kind of wanted to know," said Jackie, hoping Marcella would consent to spill some beans, "is this: Who or what is Bambi?"

"Hah." Marcella's eyes twinkled. "How'd you find out about her?"

Jackie laughed and told her the story of answering Morton Slake's private line. "It was instinctive, almost," said Jackie. "Well, I admit to being nosy. But it was more of a reflex than a conscious decision."

"I'll bet. You're lucky you didn't get caught."

Jackie looked sheepish. "I did," she said, reddening. "That was how I met Nate Northcote."

Marcella let out a huge whoop of laughter. "Seriously?"

"Yeah. Just lucky, I guess."

"I'll say. I would have picked anybody but Northcote to pop in on you in Slake's office."

"What does that mean?"

Marcella sipped at her wine, noncommittal. "Just that they're on different teams. Politics as usual. You know—for years, Slake has been quietly undermining the police department, and now he's decided to be One of Them."

Jackie shrugged. Political posturing was something that had never interested her much. Bambi, on the other hand, interested her greatly. "Do you have any idea who Bambi is?"

Marcella shook her head. "Nope. At a guess, though, I'd say she's the mistress." Marcella's green eyes sparkled with interest.

"That would be my guess," replied Jackie. She thought about Morton Slake, with his thick black hair and his perfectly cut Italian suits. "I imagine that Slake is one of those guys that figure they've got to have a mistress. Like they need a CD player or a fast car—need to keep up the image."

"One of those," agreed Marcella. "Although it's kind of weird when you think about who he's cheating on."

Jackie sat up with a start. She had completely forgotten that angle. Morton Slake's wife was none other than Marie Zug, a former beauty queen who presently was more or less of a national treasure. She had first begun to make a name for herself decorating people's houses for cocktail parties. Before long, her fame had spread among the wealthy in Palmer and its opulent suburbs. In another six months, she had prevailed on a publisher friend to give her a book contract, and—to the publisher's gratified astonishment—the book had sold a half a million copies in fifteen printings.

Marie Zug was the goddess, the mascot, and the fetish of the grown women who, as girls, had adored Barbie and her Dream House. In desperate need of a figure to worship and emulate, they had turned their cherishing eyes to Marie, who had cheerfully taught them that they were never too old to acquire the perfect life. In best-selling books and videotapes, Marie Zug told the world how to have both good taste and family harmony. For a hundred dollars, you could let your neighbors know that you had the true Christmas spirit—with a Marie Zug wreath. For twice that price, you could sleep on Marie Zug sheets, and dream the dreams that *she* dreamed. Many people considered the price a bargain.

Marie Zug was a constant guest on television talk shows, and her face had made the covers of six or seven national women's magazines. She was sacred—and now her perfect life had a blemish. Jackie commented on this irony to Marcella, who nodded in agreement.

Jackie thought over the situation. "I'll bet that's all the thieves were after—dirt on Slake. I haven't read anything about the affair in the paper. Do you think anybody really knows about her?"

"Probably Timmy Falloes—he's the one you said looked like a junior bodyguard in training. He has everything on Slake. Also, no doubt Margaret knows, since Bambi called her darling."

"I bet that tries Margaret's patience," said Jackie, thinking of the sturdy striding woman she had seen in the hall downtown. "And Nate Northcote knows. Definitely. He asked me if that was Bambi on the phone."

"Right," said Marcella thoughtfully. "And Nate Northcote."

"And now, of course, you know."

"Thanks to you," said Marcella. "It's one thing to suspect

the existence of a Bambi. It's another thing to have someone confirm it for you."

"Glad to be of service," replied Jackie with a wry smile. "Now all you have to do is make sure that Bambi's what they were after."

"What *who* were after?"

"The people that broke into your apartment."

Marcella gave this some brief thought. "Oh—well, I think she probably is. I mean, after all, a marital scandal is just what everybody wants in a boring mayoral election."

"Now Slake will have to live with zoom lenses in the bushes outside, and all of that," Jackie said with a nod. "Unless, of course, you're going to keep it quiet?"

Marcella shook her head firmly. "No. Bambi isn't really my kind of story, but I don't see any reason to keep quiet. I'm going to give her to Jerry Waters."

Jackie laughed. Jerry Waters would storm the gates of Slake's privacy in the name of Decency, and Honor, and the Public's Right to Know. He was a master of that sort of thing.

"Let's hope that Jerry Waters draws their fire."

"Why wouldn't he?" responded Marcella.

"Well, if you think about it, Bambi isn't big enough to sink Slake. I mean—the Bambis of this world make it hot for presidential candidates, but do you think the voters of Palmer will really care?"

"Hmmm."

"On the other hand, there might be something else that *would* sink him."

"Like?"

"Drugs, mayhem. Corruption. Connections with the underworld."

"Your imagination's working overtime," protested Marcella.

"No." Jackie shook her head thoughtfully. "I don't think so. Our next job is to make sure that Bambi is what they thought you had." She narrowed her eyes. "Because somebody definitely thinks you have something on Morton Slake."

CHAPTER 8

Max Greenaway, Palmer's wealthy and aristocratic commissioner of police, lived in a huge fieldstone house in Marland Gardens, the poshest residential district in the city. Greenaway was a well-known figure in Palmer, a former criminal defense lawyer, and the scion of two of the city's finest and richest old families. Shortly before the Depression, his grandmother, Jezebel Haypoint, had sold the century-old family clothing business (Haypoint Haberdashers) for close to a million dollars. In the years before WWII she had quietly invested her private fortune in steel mills and airplane engines, and in the early 1960s, against the frantic advice of her broker, she had bought large stakes in McDonald's and IBM. These shares had been sold upon her death for a breathtaking sum.

If Jezebel had lived in a more egalitarian age, she no doubt would have been a well-known figure in the financial world, as much for her clairvoyance as her fortune. But perhaps it had suited her, or amused her, to play a tame domestic role for the world around her. Everyone knew that Jezebel was well-to-do, but nobody could have guessed on what scale she had become a millionairess.

Max's grandfather was Horace Spottswood Greenaway, a firebrand who had declared Prohibition a "hypocritical

blemish on the soul of our great nation," and made a
fortune in the manufacture of bootleg liquor. When he
grew rich, Horace had also become a model of temper-
ance and piety; actually, he had never been much of a
drinker himself, but so thorough was his hatred of Prohibition that he had felt morally compelled to break the
law.

Shortly after the Repeal, he had sold his distillery (and
his secret recipes) and purchased a small daily newspaper,
the *Chronicle,* now with a circulation of 450,000. He had
also owned the Palmer Peregrines, a triple-A farm team that
kept the majors in talent; Horace had sold the Peregrines
for two million dollars shortly before his death in 1963.
"And those were 1963 dollars!" Max Greenaway was fond
of exclaiming, with a rueful, helpless shake of his head.
It wasn't Max's fault that his family was the richest in
Palmer.

It wasn't surprising, either, that Max Greenaway had
been awarded one political sinecure or another. The office
of commissioner of police, however, required not only connections but know-how; and to do the job properly it took
brains, political savvy, and the common touch. The police
forces of major cities, after all, aren't drawn from the ranks
of dilettantes, debutantes, and subscribers to chamber-music
concerts. But Max was Horace's grandson, and Horace had
known how to run with the big boys in the bootlegging business, and how to walk away unscathed when the game no
longer interested him. Most people in Palmer thought that
Max Greenaway had done a superb job as commissioner of
police.

The forty or so people who made their way to the
Greenaway house tonight for cocktails were typical of
the motley gatherings that most pleased Max. It was one
of Max's mottoes in life that it paid to be able to talk to

anyone. He had cultivated a wide friendship, with all sorts of different people.

Tonight Max and Phyllis, his wife, had invited an interesting crowd. There was an actor—really, a movie star— and two writers, one a novelist and the other a poet. There were four or five schoolteachers, because Max always felt that he could learn something new from schoolteachers; there were a couple of lawyers in private practice, and a few Wall Street types from the small but lively local brokerages. There were also, of course, a few politicians and a handful of representatives from the Palmer police force and its allies: among these was Nate Northcote.

Jackie had never been inside the Greenaway mansion, although it was a familiar landmark to her. As a white-jacketed manservant took her coat, she looked around appreciatively at the wood-paneled hall, the long graceful staircase, the enormous sliding oak doors that separated one room from the next. The house really was beautiful— perfectly proportioned, large enough to make you feel at ease here in a crowd, but not so big as to be showy. Off at the far end of the living room, in a little wood-paneled alcove, a jazz trio was playing—bass, clarinet, and keyboard.

"Nice place," she remarked under her breath to Nate. "Too bad more rich people don't have taste."

"Isn't it great?" Northcote's blue eyes shone merrily. "I get a real kick out of coming over here."

"You and Max pretty friendly, then?" Jackie asked as a waiter arrived to offer them caviar.

Northcote shrugged. "We're thrown together a lot. It helps to be on a friendly footing. Besides, I like caviar."

Nate and Jackie mixed and mingled, Nate introducing her to the people he knew, and then letting her take the ball and run with it. She appreciated his approach—they

barely knew each other, after all, and nothing irritated
Jackie more than the feeling that your date considered you
a child, unable to make conversation.

Nate obviously believed that Jackie could handle herself.
He introduced her to one person or another, then allowed
himself to be drawn off—to fill their drinks, or say hello
to a colleague. He would then return five minutes later and scoop her up. Obviously, thought Jackie wryly,
he'd had a lot of practice. Still, practice makes perfect,
and she had decided that Nate Northcote was behaving
perfectly.

Jackie, who had lived for so many years away from
Palmer, was earnestly delighted to find herself becoming
a part, once more, of the varied social life of the city. She
looked around at the guests, some of whom she knew, and
realized that never could she have found such a pleasant
mixture in Kingswood. From a spot near the garden door,
she eyed Nate across the room, deep in conversation with a
tall, dark-haired woman in a blue dress. With surprise and
satisfaction, she recognized Jane Bellamy, a fellow faculty
member at Rodgers.

Jane Bellamy was opposing Morton Slake in the race for
mayor, and everyone knew that the incumbent mayor had
backed Slake. Not twenty feet away, Jackie caught sight of
Morton Slake himself, looking slightly out of his depth. No
doubt he had been thrown off his guard by the presence of
Jane Bellamy. At his side hovered the puffy-lipped young
man whom Jackie thought of as the "junior bodyguard."
Jackie laughed quietly to herself. Max Greenaway, although
a mayor's appointee, was evidently his own man.

"Scoping out the crowd?" asked a voice in her ear.

Jackie whirled to see Cosmo Gordon. She grinned broad-
ly and gave him a warm hug.

"Cosmo! It's been ages!"

"Not exactly ages, my dear," he responded warmly. "More like two months. I guess Michael has been keeping you all to himself." He took Jackie's elbow and guided her gently out of the way. Morton Slake was passing through. Jackie laughed to see him bowing to left and right, like the Queen Mother. The junior bodyguard followed solemnly a few steps behind his master. The procession of two came to rest about three feet from Jackie and Cosmo, who did their best not to laugh.

"Michael? Oh, he turns up from time to time. But he never brings you along. Why don't you come? You could at least stick your head in the door to say hello to Jake."

"Good old Jake. We never should have let that one retire. Too much talent, of which the police are in desperate need. How is the old guy?"

"He's fine. He and Peter have become totally inseparable, which is good and bad. Peter refuses to understand why Jake can't go to school with him."

Gordon scratched his head, pondering. "Well, to be honest, I don't see why either. A well-trained dog like that would probably be able to give lessons in good manners to half the children in the class."

"He would, wouldn't he?" Jackie grinned. "Not a single one of them can shake hands properly. But Jake could show them."

Cosmo's eyes roved around the room, and Jackie knew he was trying to puzzle out why, and with whom, she was here. She let him look for a minute or so; eventually his eyes rested on Nate, who was still talking to Jane Bellamy.

Jackie dodged the question in Cosmo's eyes. "You and Max know each other from work, I guess?" she asked innocently.

"Funny—no, not really. We sort of coast along in different grooves—I tell the detectives what I think, and so does

Max." Cosmo Gordon chuckled. "No, seriously—I know him better through my wife, Nancy. She's quite close to Phyllis. Nancy's a pianist." Cosmo's eyes rested on a small, neat-looking, dark-haired woman across the room, who was talking to their hostess. "Not professional, not any longer. But still a musician, of course."

Jackie followed Cosmo's glance. Phyllis Greenaway had been a flautist with the Palmer Symphony for many years. She looked somehow like a flautist, thought Jackie—tall and thin, with a long wispy braid of golden hair that had just begun to go gray. She was wearing some kind of Turkish-looking thing, long and purple and utterly becoming; she was the kind of woman who could make a caftan look beautiful. On most women, Jackie reflected, that purple thing would have been worse than a potato sack.

"From what I hear," she commented, "it's typical of Max Greenaway to have married talent, rather than money."

"I'd agree with that," replied Gordon. "Although you can never be sure about people. Maybe Phyllis is rich too."

"That would make it nicer for *her,* I think," said Jackie. "Not having to feel like a poor relation."

"Well—everybody's a poor relation when you stack 'em up against the Greenaway fortune. But you know, Max is okay. It couldn't have happened to a nicer person."

Nate had joined them, a smile on his face, and he stuck out a hand to Cosmo.

"Long time, Doctor. Long time."

Cosmo Gordon shook hands, with less than his usual warmth, thought Jackie. "Hello, Nate. Good to see you."

"You and Jackie have met, I see?"

"We're old friends," said Gordon, his voice careful and noncommittal. "Finished with that Genner case, Nate?"

Northcote accepted the change of topic with gentlemanly smoothness. "Funny—no, we haven't. Nowhere near ready for trial. In fact, I was going to call you about it next week."

They talked shop for a few moments, and Jackie listened carefully, trying not to let too much interest show. It seemed to her that there was something strained between the two men, and the sensation made her uncomfortable. Although she didn't know Cosmo Gordon all that well, somehow his being Michael McGowan's close friend and mentor made him above any kind of suspicion or reproach. Yet if she wasn't mistaken, Nate Northcote didn't seem to trust him or like him.

She listened to them talk about the Genner case, whatever it was. Probably they had had some kind of disagreement over forensic evidence, thought Jackie. Probably Cosmo had said one thing about some bullet wound, or time of death, when Nate wanted the evidence to point in another direction. That sort of thing must happen a lot.

In another moment, Nancy Gordon had joined them, and the conversation became general once more. Cosmo was casual in making his introductions, but Nancy Gordon registered a flash of recognition when he pronounced her name, and Jackie felt a pang of guilt. Was it her imagination? Or did Nancy look at her with a trace of hurt surprise? Did Nancy and Cosmo look on Jackie as Michael's girl, the way everybody else seemed to?

Jackie felt some slight relief when they left the cocktail party. Nate suggested dinner at Suki's Place, downtown, and Jackie agreed instantly. Something about the encounter with Cosmo and Nancy—or something in the encounter between Nate and Cosmo—had left a funny feeling behind. Jackie was eager to wash it away, to get back on a fresh footing with Nate. She hoped it would be possible.

Suki's was undoubtedly the best restaurant in Palmer. It wasn't the most expensive, although it was pricey enough to keep most people at arm's length; Jackie couldn't remember when she'd last had a meal here. It must have been three or four years ago, on one of her periodic flights from the suburbs.

The place hadn't changed much—still the same soft lighting, elegant white tablecloths, perfect flowers, understated but interesting artwork on the walls. Still the same peaceful air—not hushed or drearily reverential—merry, but not noisy. It was perfect.

Sidney, the maître d', gave Nate a familiar nod and spoke to him briefly in a quiet voice, while Jackie waited. Tall, gray-haired, handsome, and distinguished-looking, Sidney was pretty much of a Palmer tradition; he had been working at Suki's for at least two decades, and perhaps longer. It was clear from his manner that Nate Northcote was a frequent diner. He must have money somewhere, thought Jackie. Nobody could come to Suki's very often on a civil servant's salary.

Over braised endive with goat cheese, Nate told Jackie the story of his life—the selected bits, at any rate. He had a lively way of talking that seemed pleasantly at odds with his lankiness; Jackie found his high spirits all the more engaging because they were unexpected.

Nate had been married, he told her, to a beautiful but restless woman named Camilla; after a few years of leading a very ordinary life in Palmer, she had run away with the owner of a tiny island in the Caribbean. Her new home, Nate told Jackie with a smile, was a place where the very wealthy went to dwell briefly in rough huts of untrammeled simplicity, to live by the lights of kerosene lanterns before going home in their private jets.

On Santo Argelio, Camilla was still presumably baking in the sun and learning from the servants new ways to combine fish with lime juice. There wasn't much on the island, except the lime trees, and the lagoon with its fish, and the native population—three hundred strong—who hired themselves out as cooks and porters and maids. Primitive living is much more fun, Nate pointed out with a smile, if someone else hauls your water up from the well.

"Your wife's island sounds okay to me," said Jackie.

"Forever?"

"God, no!" She looked horrified. "I mean, going off with rich people for a week or two."

"Yes, I admit that part sounds like fun. Plenty of help, and yet you have that nice satisfying exhaustion at the end of the day that comes from fresh air, from tying your own shoes. No TV, no hot tub, you can't even run down to the casino to play baccarat."

Jackie laughed. "I loved summer camp as a girl. For many of the same reasons."

"But when you grew up, you gave up gambling."

"I don't play baccarat, at least. Too rich for my blood."

"I never did much like Monte Carlo," rejoined Nate with a smile.

The waiter arrived with the wine: a moment of truth. You could easily be obliged to cross a man off your list if he responded poorly to the challenge.

Jackie was relieved and pleased with the way Nate handled the test. He merely sipped and nodded, barely allowing the arrival of the wine to interrupt his flow of conversation. No flash of academic seriousness crossed his brow; Jackie suddenly decided that she liked him very much.

When the fish arrived—Suki's had the best grilled sole that Jackie had ever tasted—Nate began to ask for information in exchange. "I've told you mine. Fair's fair."

Jackie agreed. It felt good, in a way, to talk about Cooper, to compare Camilla's flight to Santo Argelio and Cooper's entrenchment in the Kingswood Country Club. Insular lives for people who liked being insular.

"And you like being back in Palmer?"

"I adore it. Luckily, so does my son, Peter."

"Let me guess . . . fourth grade?"

"Fifth—he just turned eleven. At the doorway to some rough years, I'm afraid."

"You'll manage."

It was said with such warmth and confidence that as she tucked into her sole, Jackie actually believed that she would. She and Petey would manage. She and Petey and Jake. With relish, Jackie told Nate Northcote Jake's history—how he had appeared on their doorstep, exhausted and bleeding, and how, after many weeks, they had discovered that he had once been a police dog. "When I found that out, I was terrified," she said. "I thought he might turn on us, or go all strange. But he's an excellent family dog, and we'd be completely lost without him. He's not what you'd call cute—more like handsome and dignified. But he and Peter are inseparable."

"You say he used to work for the K-9 squad?" asked Northcote lightly.

Jackie nodded. "But that was a long time ago. He had a few years of retirement in there, I think. Adapted himself to family living, I guess."

"Huh." Northcote looked thoughtful. "Happen to remember the name of the people he used to belong to?"

"No, I don't," replied Jackie easily, reaching for her wineglass.

It was nearing midnight when Jackie and Nate Northcote arrived back at the loft on Isabella Lane. The evening had been a long one, and extremely pleasant, with only one false note.

Why had she lied to Nate?

For of course she knew exactly who Jake's former owner had been. Matt Dugan was the man's name. He was an ex-cop, and he had been a good friend of Cosmo Gordon's, and he had been murdered in the seedy little alley behind Leanna's Piano Parlor. And as far as she knew, the police were still looking for the killer. And, probably, Nate Northcote knew all about the case. He was, after all, the senior prosecuting attorney. If the case ever came to trial, he'd be in charge of it. But Michael had once warned her that it was best to keep quiet about Jake, and his advice had stayed in the back of her mind.

As she said a polite but warm good night to Nate, Jackie suddenly recalled the funny, stiff way that Cosmo Gordon had greeted Nate. It had to be just business, thought Jackie. It must be. She put Cosmo Gordon resolutely out of her mind, and smiled at Northcote. He responded with a warm grin that made her very glad, all of a sudden, that she'd been caught snooping in Morton Slake's office.

"I had thought that maybe one of these Saturdays you and Peter would like to go for a little jaunt in the country. Please say yes."

Jackie smiled. "Only if we can bring our dog with us. We never go anywhere without Jake, especially on Saturdays."

"Of course Jake can come. In fact, he's helping me with the planning. For next Saturday, at ten in the morning. He has it all worked out."

And so it was settled. Nate said good night, and Jackie, exhausted, was halfway to the kitchen, looking for Jake, before she remembered that he had gone to spend the night at Isaac's house with Peter.

The red light on the answering machine in the hall was blinking. With a yawn, Jackie rewound and listened.

Two hang-up calls. Peter ("Hi, Mom!"). Marcella Jacobs wanting to play tennis. Another hang-up call. Cosmo Gordon.

Jackie frowned and rewound the tape to listen to Cosmo's message again. She looked at her watch—nearly twelve. Well, she could hear what Cosmo had to say in the morning. That would be soon enough.

CHAPTER 9

"I don't ordinarily do this kind of thing, Jackie," said Gordon, standing apologetically before her. It was early on Saturday morning, and Jackie was in the kitchen of her loft, awaiting Jake's and Peter's return from Isaac's house. Cosmo Gordon had appeared a minute or so ago, while Jackie was making cookie dough. She had been pleasantly recalling some of last night's high points. There was no question that she liked Nate Northcote a great deal.

And then Cosmo Gordon had come, breaking into her pleasant reverie and forcing her to recollect the stiffness, the uneasiness, that she had witnessed between them last night. She felt cheated, all of a sudden.

Jackie glared at Gordon. "If you don't usually do this sort of thing, then I don't think you need to start now." She knew she sounded intolerant, even rude. But, after all, her private life was none of this man's business. Suddenly she was heartily sick and tired of Michael McGowan and all of his friends, and all of those kind, well-meaning, intrusive people who seemed to think that she belonged to Michael somehow—or he to her. Good heavens, it was getting to be a virtual prison. She waited impatiently for Cosmo's response. Maybe he would feel hurt and rejected, and just go.

"I'm here only because I like you. I want you to be safe and out of harm's way."

A father figure, protecting her from unscrupulous suitors. That was something Jackie did not feel she needed. She bridled at the thought. "Oh, honestly, Cosmo—"

"Please. Just hear me out, Jackie, and then I'll go, and leave you in peace with your chocolate-chip cookies."

Jackie began to relent a bit. After all, the man was a good, kind, honest person, and a good friend to Michael. She owed him a hearing. Then she could shoo him out.

"All right. I'm sorry I snapped at you—I didn't mean to be rude." But she was still angry, and perched restlessly on the edge of her chair, ready to leap up and send Cosmo Gordon packing if he became too avuncular.

"No offense taken." Gordon studied Jackie's restless, defensive posture, then settled himself comfortably in a chair opposite her. She provided him with a mug of coffee. He studied her and took a thoughtful sip. "I'll start at the beginning. It won't take long."

Jackie had expected Gordon's tale to be one built along personal, romantic lines. She prepared to hear the information that Nate Northcote had four wives, or that he was a well-known heartbreaker, or that he had jilted Gordon's daughter, or anything. But Cosmo surprised her. He talked about work. He talked about homicide. He talked about the murder of Matt Dugan, ex-cop.

The story that he told Jackie was already, in parts, familiar to her. But there were things that she hadn't known. He related the progress—or lack of it—in finding any kind of evidence that would lead the police to the murderer. He told her that it had begun to look like the detective division would have to shelve the case. Except for one thing, which he and Michael had discovered by accident earlier in the week. They had found the gun—they had traced it, by

sheer luck. It was a gun that had been used and recovered
in another recent shooting.

"Michael and I were talking about it on Tuesday. I should
thank you, by the way, for the help you gave us last
week."

"Me?"

Gordon nodded. "The lab results that we needed. That we
couldn't have asked for ourselves without arousing some
kind of suspicion. Or, at the very least, curiosity."

"I see." Jackie suddenly felt very nervous. She thought
perhaps Cosmo was leading to some unpleasant revelations.

"Yes—there are difficulties. This case is tremendously
sensitive, Jackie," he said, as if reading her thoughts. "Both
Michael and I feel that there has been obstruction of the
investigation by members of the department."

Jackie was silent for a moment, letting this sink in. If
it was true, both Cosmo and Michael could be exposing
themselves to all sorts of reprisals—if anyone found out
what they were after.

On the other hand, Michael had told her about Cosmo's
long friendship with Dugan, and his guilt over not being
able to save his friend from himself. She thought about
this. Wasn't it probable that Cosmo was becoming
a little obsessed? Surely that was more likely than
the Palmer police joining together in a conspiracy
of silence. Gordon sat silently while Jackie thought it all
through.

"Well, Cosmo—look," she said at last. "I don't really
know how to say this politely—"

"That's quite all right, Jackie. Just say it."

"All right. Don't you think maybe that the department is
just trying to dissociate itself from a—a dishonest member
of the force? Maybe that's the reason that the investigation
is dragging along so slowly."

Gordon shook his head. "I wish that were true, Jackie. Honestly I do. I'm not on a personal mission here, although it may seem that way. Matt Dugan was my friend—but the department cut him out over ten years ago when he was kicked off the force. The fact that he was discharged says it all. There is nothing about his killing that could drag the police down—unless there was some truth to the things he was nattering on about the last time I saw him."

"What things?"

Gordon sighed. "I wish I had listened more carefully to him. He was trembling, and his clothes were a wreck, and he looked pathetic, when he came to our house. He came to the door quite unexpectedly, but of course we were glad to see him anyway. He stayed for dinner with us, and Nancy treated him like a member of the family, a long-lost cousin or something. When he left, I walked him to the bus to make sure he got on it all right—oh, it was hard to see a friend in such distress! And while we waited for the bus, he told me that he had found out some things that would make the mayor and the commissioner reinstate him in the department. He said he had evidence of some kind of criminal wrongdoing, corruption, bribe-taking, and so forth."

"And you thought he was just spouting."

"That's right." Gordon looked stricken. "Well, they were just the kinds of things you might expect a disgruntled, disgraced ex-cop to say. All about how he was going to prove to the world that he still could be a good cop, even though he had let the department down before. He was going to vindicate himself by breaking a ring of corruption, single-handed. And so forth and so on. I didn't really listen to him, Jackie, because it hurt too much to hear him go on like that."

"I can imagine."

"And then he was killed, you know. Three days later."

"And you began to wonder about the things he'd told you."

Gordon nodded. "He was murdered in cold blood, and the department has been dragging its heels for nine months on the case. Officially, there is absolutely nothing, so far. But, because I was worried, I had a look through the files. So has Michael—although it's as much as his job is worth to go sneaking a look through Stillman's files."

"Who's Stillman?"

"The new captain in homicide. He was promoted in November, a week after Matt was killed."

Something in Gordon's tone made Jackie uneasy. "Well, surely, Cosmo, you don't think there's a connection?" Jackie had again begun to think that Gordon was rambling. She had never put much stock in conspiracy theories—in a small way, she had rebelled against her own generation. It was much easier to believe in laziness or weakness of will than in a deliberate, active conspiracy of evil.

Gordon, by way of an answer, smiled absently. He had thought long and hard about Evan Stillman. He had disagreed, at first, with McGowan's assessment of the situation—it was no secret that Stillman's promotion meant that Michael's own chances were slimmer. McGowan loathed him quietly, but did his bidding—he had no wish to abbreviate his own career through arousing the ire of his new captain.

Stillman was the kind of person who never read between the lines, never lifted his head to look around out of curiosity. He approached his cases with a total lack of imagination; McGowan sometimes wondered how anything was resolved at all. Stillman had moved up the ranks merely by virtue of playing the game. He seemed to have incredible breaks, like a man on a parcheesi board who rolled double sixes all the time. In Michael McGowan's estimate—and Cosmo Gordon had come to share his young friend's point of view—Stillman wasn't really a cop. He was just a bureaucrat who had happened to join the Palmer force.

But given Stillman's character, it was no surprise that he hadn't strained himself on the Dugan case. It was just the kind of thing that Stillman would despise. The story of Dugan's fall from grace was a cautionary tale, and Evan Stillman hadn't needed a warning. He did everything by the book. No need to lift rocks to see what was crawling around underneath.

Cosmo Gordon explained all of this to Jackie, as best he could without exposing too much about Michael McGowan's private on-the-job struggles. Gordon described how he had come to agree with McGowan's evaluation of the new homicide captain. Stillman hadn't the heart or the soul to command police officers in the line of duty, to understand the twisted passions and burning desires that led people to break the law in the first place. And he certainly hadn't the nerve to ruffle anyone's feathers by pressing too hard on an uncomfortable matter.

"So what *has* he done?" asked Jackie.

"That's just what we're trying to assess, Michael and I. And that's where we've had a lucky break. Thanks to you."

"Me?"

"The other day, Michael gave you photocopies of two lab reports. The information in each looked similar to us, but we're no experts when it comes to ballistics evidence. The good people in the Hertz Laboratory are, however. The technician who made the comparison for us agreed that the bullets came from the same gun."

"You mean that the department *has* traced the gun that was used to kill Matt Dugan?" All of a sudden, Jackie didn't understand what the big deal was. Stillman, no matter how much Michael and Cosmo disliked him, had done his job. It had begun to sound as though Cosmo and Michael just had an ax to grind.

Gordon read her thoughts. "Yes and no, my dear." He smiled, and Jackie felt a wave of guilt wash over her. These were her good friends whose word she was doubting.

Cosmo Gordon went on. "We have the lab reports. We know that the gun that killed Matt Dugan has been traced. But on Thursday, Michael talked to one of the detectives assigned to the Dugan case and told him that the gun had been traced—that it was in fact evidence in another shooting. And that it was right in the police property room."

"Well, that's a relief, then, isn't it?"

"Right. This detective went back to get the gun on Friday morning, and guess what?"

"No."

"Right. Gone."

"Yikes."

"So, my dear, you see that I am not just a heartbroken, guilt-wracked old man."

"Cosmo."

He smiled to lessen the impact of his words. "This has, all of a sudden, become a very dangerous game. It's one thing to fight the criminals on the outside. It's a whole different ball game when you can't trust your fellow police officers. Michael may be in grave danger—of losing his job, at least, if not his life. These people are not fooling around."

"And you think," said Jackie, finally understanding why Gordon was here, "that Nate Northcote is in on it too?"

Gordon looked uncomfortable. "I don't know what to think. I only know that it's no secret that you're a friend of Michael's. The murder at Rodgers last fall was big news, and your role in it was made quite clear."

"But that has nothing to do with—"

"It's also evident, I think, that you're a friend of mine. Jackie, Michael and I are extremely uneasy about the Dugan case. We are dismayed by the implications of everything we have seen so far."

"And you're worried about me." Jackie was struck by the kindness of Gordon's concern. He hadn't liked to stick his nose into her personal business. But he had done so.

"I am, a little. It's possible that if there's any funny business in the department, it may also be present in the prosecuting attorney's office. I want you to be aware of that fact. Your friendship with me and Michael may put you in jeopardy, you know, if there's really something wrong. We won't be able to protect you. Far from it."

Jackie felt suddenly very ill at ease.

Nate Northcote seemed like a nice man—amusing, intelligent, and all the rest. She wanted very much to believe that he had nothing to do with Michael and Cosmo's dilemma. She wanted, in fact, to believe that there was no problem in the Palmer police force—that whatever difficulty there was in apprehending the murderer of Matt Dugan was the result of inefficiency, or lack of interest, or laziness—anything but deliberate malice.

Something of her apprehension must have shown on her face, for Cosmo responded with sympathy.

"He's a very agreeable man, is Nate Northcote. I've always liked him."

"You always used to like him, you mean," replied Jackie, not without humor, "until you found out that he's either a murderer, or a corrupt lawyer, or both."

Gordon sighed. "Right now, Jackie, there isn't anybody connected with Matt's death that I can trust."

"But how is Nate connected?" There was an edge of protest in Jackie's voice. She didn't believe in guilt by association. Just because a few detectives were bad didn't mean the P.A. was in cahoots with them. "I don't get it."

"No. I haven't told you, have I?" Gordon closed his eyes thoughtfully and took in a deep breath. He was quiet a moment, and Jackie felt her heart begin to race. Gordon spoke again.

"On Friday morning, Max Greenaway issued a directive to suspend temporarily the investigation into Matt's death."

"Oh. And you think it's not just a coincidence."

"I don't see how it could be."

"Well—what kind of excuse did they give?"

"Max cited the lack of evidence. Late Friday afternoon, I called him up and asked him about it, and he said he was acting on Nate's recommendation. Nate had seen all the files and decided that there was nothing in it for the office of Palmer's prosecuting attorney. Max seemed to agree, and said there were more pressing cases."

"He closed it?"

"No. You never close a homicide case. But if there's nobody working on it, the case is as good as dead. Nobody will be reassigned to it, unless there's some hard evidence."

"But what about the gun? You'll find it, and then that will be evidence."

"I doubt we'll find it. It was stolen from the police property office—a pretty blatant example of concealing evidence."

"Maybe it was taken for some other reason. Something connected with the other shooting."

Gordon frowned at Jackie, and her heart sank. She realized how unlikely that was. The only thing that had changed the status quo, regarding that gun, was its connection to the death of Matt Dugan. Obviously.

"Well, what about the lab report I got for you the other day? Doesn't that count as evidence?"

Cosmo Gordon shook his head. "Without the gun, my dear, we have nothing. The files have been cleaned out. All we have are the photocopies of the ballistics reports in two unrelated shootings. The photocopies are ones that Michael made; they haven't been notarized and could never be introduced as evidence. Even if we could make Northcote's office believe that there was a link, they wouldn't touch the photocopies."

Jackie watched Cosmo Gordon go with a heavy heart. It wasn't as though she was in love with Nate Northcote—far from it. But she had thought him lovable; in the aftermath of her marriage and divorce, the idea that a man could be lovable had comforted her, in some remote way.

But that was over with now. Cosmo Gordon's revelations had made it impossible to think of Nate Northcote as anything but a smooth operator. Somehow that was worse, for Jackie, than thinking of him as an out-and-out criminal. It was depressing to think that he had put one over on her—with his charm and his blue eyes and his warm, easy smile. She was angry with herself for not being more cautious.

She thought again about the way he had questioned her last night. His banter about Jake had been light—but had there been something behind it? He must know that Jackie had Matt Dugan's dog. And, knowing that, why hadn't he said so? Why had he pretended not to know?

As she looked the situation over, in the new light shed by Cosmo's information, the conversation about Jake appeared almost sinister. It was just possible that Nate suspected her

of having some stronger connection with Matt Dugan—
after all, people didn't ordinarily go around taking in stray
dogs whose owners were murder victims.

Who was a witness to the fact that her friendship with
Jake had preceded her friendship with Michael? Who would
tell Matt Dugan's murderer that she, Jackie Walsh, had
never known the man whose dog she had adopted? That
she had no ax to grind?

Who would protect her, and Peter, and Jake, from the
people who had gunned down Matt Dugan in cold blood?

At least she hadn't admitted to Nate, last night, that she
knew Matt Dugan, or anything about him. Maybe nobody
would ever figure it out. She and Peter would be safe.

Again, Jackie puzzled over the lie she had told Nate last
night. Where had the lie come from?

Perhaps she was more sensitive, on a certain level, than
she realized. After all, there had been no reason to hold
out on him—not last night. And yet she had lied, straight
out lied, as easy as rolling off a log. There must have been
some reason for it, some subconscious prompting.

Had she been protecting herself? Or Cosmo, and by
extension Michael?

Well, that didn't matter. What mattered now was getting
to the bottom of this problem. Either Nate Northcote was
guilty or he was innocent. Either way, Jackie intended to
keep her next date with him.

She sat back and tried to look at the question objectively.
She considered herself, by now, a fairly skilled investigator—after all, she had helped Michael McGowan solve two
very difficult cases. One way or another, she would get to
the bottom of this one too. It wouldn't do to sit at home and
worry that a gang of murderers might come after them. The
only way to feel safe again, and on certain ground, was to
find the truth of the situation.

Was she involving herself for her own sake? Or Nate's? Or Michael's?

The answer to that question would be part of the truth, as well.

CHAPTER 10

Late Saturday afternoon, reworking the reconstruction of her interviews and notes on the Slake profile, Marcella Jacobs began to feel satisfied. It was the first time in a long time that she had felt on top of things—the first time since the break-in at her apartment.

Reconstructing the interviews from memory had been a laborious job; even now she wasn't sure it would turn out to have been worth the effort. But she had gone too far with this business to give up on it now, and if she didn't write her story, it might be years before anybody hit on the truth. Certainly nothing would be revealed before the election, and that was what counted, after all.

Marcella Jacobs was well trained and blessed with a strong memory for details. Over the course of a week, she had managed to reconstruct the substance of most of her notes. The reconstruction was useless, of course, from a journalistic standpoint, but at least it gave her a jumping-off point. There was no reason to think that most of what she'd done was permanently lost.

She had spent a long week reconstructing interviews; her plan was to go back to the subjects and ask them for a simple confirmation, a simple yes or no, on the substance of the interviews. *Does this agree with your recollection or not? Sign here, please.*

The problem with her plan was that it gave the subjects, in effect, editorial control. But it was either that or go through with a pointless charade of interviewing them all over again. Because without her notes, her recollection of the interviews would be worthless. But if she started all over again, from scratch, they would be on their guard. At least one of them would, anyway.

There was only one person on her list of interview subjects that bothered her. She had worked and reworked the substance of that conversation, trying very hard not to make it look as though the talk had led anywhere in particular, to any specific conclusion. As she glanced once more through the encapsulation of the interview, she reckoned that she had done fairly well. Now she just needed a little dumb luck on her side.

Peter Walsh was not the kind of boy to get nervous about things. He had his father's red hair but not the volatility that often went with it; Peter's temperament disposed him to manifest a rocklike stolidity in the face of strange occurrences.

At times, Peter's friend Isaac Cook considered him too much of a realist—he never, for example, could be frightened by ghost stories or by being forced to stick his hand in the dish of "eyeballs" at a spook house. When Peter and Isaac went to the movies, Peter—quick to disbelief—analyzed the special effects. He rarely succumbed to them. This was just the way Peter was, dispassionate and inclined to skepticism.

Real crime, on the other hand, was something that Peter usually took very seriously indeed. Perhaps it was his friendship with Michael McGowan, or his pride in Jake's magnificent training, that made him constantly on the look-

out for wrongdoers. He had a keen eye and a realistic sense
of right and wrong.

Thus when Peter came home late on Saturday afternoon
and told his mother that a strange man had been following
him, she took him at his word. Peter was not a boy to make
such things up, to make mountains out of molehills.

"Tell me all about it, Petey," Jackie commanded as she
took the oatmeal cookies from the oven. "Everything. What
happened?"

"Well, me and Isaac—"

"Tell me in English, please." Jackie rolled her eyes.
It was a constant struggle, and not even an emergency
could dampen her instinct to make Peter master his native
language. "Isaac and I."

"Isaac and I were in the park with Jake. We were throwing a tennis ball for him, but you know he doesn't really
like to fetch." Jackie nodded. She thought Jake was awfully
forbearing, at times. Heaven knew that it was certainly
beneath his dignity to fetch. He clearly believed that he
had been born for greater things than retrieving.

"So anyway," Peter went on, "there was this guy kind of
watching us. At first I didn't really notice him too much,
but he had a newspaper and he never turned the page over.
You know?"

Jackie knew.

There were a hundred and one different, equally unap-
pealing reasons why a strange man might be watching her
little boy. Jackie tried not to jump to conclusions. Her hand
was trembling as she transferred the oatmeal cookies, one
by one, onto a plate, where they sagged and settled in, their
sides touching.

"Isaac noticed him first, really, but Isaac is kind of like
that. Said he thought the guy looked like a Russian spy."

Jackie nodded. Where Peter was realistic, his friend Isaac

was full of invention. Peter went on. "But he stuck around for a real long time, so then I decided to keep my eye on him. He was only pretending to read the newspaper. That was easy to see."

"Did he try to talk to you?"

"Yup. He *did* talk to us. Well, he tried to talk to Jake."

"To Jake?"

"Yeah. Whistled for him. So Isaac says, 'He's not really very friendly,' the guy says something about maybe he'll teach him how to shake hands. Wanted us all to watch while he taught Jake how to shake hands." Peter rolled his eyes. As if such juvenile tricks held even the slightest challenge for Jake—who could put most competitors to shame.

"What did Jake do?"

"He kind of looked at him and lowered his tail, the way he does when he doesn't like somebody. But he didn't growl or anything. He didn't really seem to care about the guy."

Jackie puzzled over this for a minute. Perhaps the man had been harmless. She herself often talked to strange dogs.

Peter reached absently for a cookie. Still hot, it sagged and broke in half. He blew on the half that remained in his hand, took a bite, and went on. "The guy kind of reminded me of that friend of Grandma's who kept wanting me to recite my lines from the school play. Remember?"

Jackie did remember—a dreary neighbor of her mother's who thought he had a "way" with children. He had actually gone so far as to chuck Peter under the chin. Peter had loathed the man on sight, and with good reason.

"Then what happened, Petey? Did you talk to him?"

"No way." Peter was firm. He knew what was expected of him in these circumstances. What was more, he didn't generally waste his time satisfying the demands of dweeby adults. Not that he was ever rude. But being an only child, and finding himself frequently in the company of adults whom he thought tiresome, he had long ago developed a knack for turning people away with a polite, remote, utterly irreproachable stare. Jackie envied him this talent and the discrimination that went with it. She often thought she was far too nice to people. Before she knew it, they had a toehold in her life. Even if it wasn't, necessarily, a good idea.

That thought reminded her of Nate Northcote, and she felt a momentary unease. "Is that it? Or is there more?"

Peter scowled briefly at his mother. Peter had not exaggerated. So far, there had been no following in the story. Obviously there was more. "I told you he followed us."

"So you did. Go on." Jackie helped herself to a cookie.

"Okay. So, I whistled for Jake, and Isaac and I talked it over and decided we would both go to Billy Bishop's house."

"Why Billy's?"

"Because he lives right near the park. Plus, his father works nights and is home during the day and he's really big and mean-looking."

"Excellent reasoning. And?"

"So we went over there and hung out with Billy for a half an hour or so. Then we thought we'd go home. But the guy was there, on the sidewalk."

Jackie felt a chill. Who was this creature who was stalking her child? "What did you do?"

"We got Billy's mom to wake up Mr. Bishop." Peter's eyes lit up. "He grabbed Billy's baseball bat and opened the door and just stared at the guy. The guy took off."

Jackie felt nervous.

Obviously, the man had reasoned that Isaac and Peter—Isaac with his coal-black hair and dark skin, his twinkling dark eyes—were not brothers. Not being brothers, they would have to part, eventually, on their way home.

And then he would get—which one? Peter? Or Isaac? What did he want with her little boy?

It didn't matter. Whatever the man was after, he had better watch his step.

She reached for the phone and dialed Michael McGowan.

"Female Caucasian. Age about thirty-six. Dressed in a raincoat, slacks, a dark turtleneck." The voice was flat and mechanical; the information was nothing new. This type of thing, the voice in the floodlit darkness seemed to say, well, this type of thing happens. "Strangled. With the belt from the raincoat."

The warm, thin rain came down steadily, visible in the headlights, softening the sounds of the conversation. Flickering brilliant red and blue lights created a brittle, festive air.

Practiced hands groped through the soaking wet raincoat pockets, turning them inside-out. Trouser pockets. Pocketbook. Fingers felt in the dark for jewelry—hands, earlobes, neck, wrists.

"Okay," said the first voice. "Call her in, Mason."

"Right."

Heavy shoes crunched across wet, gravelly sand. A car door opened, and there came the muffled squawk of a radio. "Six-nine-three-four to University Precinct. Come in. Over. Right. Lieutenant McGowan, Jack Mason here. Yes. Forty-two block of Kennedy. Presumed homicide. Over."

CHAPTER 11

"So you mean she never showed up?" Jackie asked Marcella Jacobs.

The two women were sitting on one of the old wood-and-wrought-iron benches alongside the Little Field in Holcomb Park. Before them, in grass that was still wet from last night's long rainstorm, Peter and Isaac and Jake were rushing back and forth between balled-up sweatshirts on the ground. To Jackie it appeared to be a makeshift game of base runners—a difficult game to play if only two of the three players could throw. Somehow the boys had worked out a system, something elaborate having to do with which way Jake was facing when the ball was thrown, or whether he was sitting down, or something. She had given up trying to figure out the system.

Since hearing Peter's tale yesterday of the man in the park watching them, Jackie had decided that the boys could use a friendly eye. For the next few days, at least, until whoever he was decided to pick on someone else. Sarah Cook, Isaac's mother, had agreed with Jackie's assessment. Isaac's version of the event had, predictably, been much more colorful and enlarged than Peter's, but it had been substantially the same. Both boys had provided a fairly complete description of the man: tall, dark-haired, in a blue shirt with a hole in the breast pocket, blue jeans, and loafers. Thin. They thought he had blue eyes.

Determining his age had proved difficult for the boys. Peter had pegged him as "pretty old—probably even older than you, Mom"; whereas Isaac had characterized him as "pretty old, but not as old as my mom." These estimates were not at all helpful, since Sarah Cook and Jackie Walsh were more or less the same age. Thus—bruised egos aside—it was a difficult call. Jackie put him somewhere between thirty and forty-five. Some help.

The description, of course, fit Nate Northcote perfectly.

She could picture him in jeans and loafers and a blue shirt with a hole at the pocket—a ratty old button-down oxford-cloth shirt, too beat-up for office wear, but just reaching that degree of softness that makes a shirt perfect to put on. Tall and thin and dark-haired, watching her boy in the park, with an amused twinkle in his slate-blue eyes. Why?

It was Sunday afternoon, a bright hot day, with plenty of heat and daylight left. Marcella had called just as Jackie and Peter had been leaving the house, and she had tagged along, evidently in need of company. She was feeling frustrated, professionally: Bambi, Morton Slake's presumed mistress, had scheduled a very promising interview with Marcella, and then she had failed to show up.

"Bambi just didn't make it?"

"No," replied Marcella, "and she didn't call to cancel or anything. I think it's a little bit weird."

"Probably she just lost her nerve," Jackie suggested.

"I doubt it. She didn't seem the type. Besides, she's the one who called me, after all."

"So you said. But I thought you were going to give her to Jerry Waters. Make her this week's item on *Your Right to Know*."

Marcella shook her head. "I tried. Apparently she had

already told Jerry to go jump in a lake, or something like that."

"That's strange." Jackie dug a sneakered toe in the gluey mud at their feet. The rain yesterday evening had been steady and heavy. "Usually, if they want to talk, they want to get on Jerry's show."

"Yeah. Generally speaking, I think Jerry is much more up their alley—up the alley of disgruntled mistresses of public figures."

"More high profile."

"Exactly."

They sat in silence awhile, contemplating the world of disgruntled mistresses of public figures. To Jackie, there was something pathetic about the Bambis of this world, who risked a lot and then ended up losing. The problem with people like Morton Slake was that they had no loyalty— none to their wives, and even less to their mistresses.

"So how did you get in touch with her? Put out a personal ad saying, 'Bambi, phone me'?"

"She got my name from Jerry. Seems he dug her up on his own, but he couldn't talk her into coming on the show. Sometimes he's really kind of a jerk," Marcella added thoughtfully. "But I think he knew she might have a good story for me, and that he'd let me have a crack at it, since she refused to talk to him."

"So she called you. When?"

"Friday. We agreed to meet last night at the Pancake Palace on Kennedy. I waited for three hours."

"When she called you, did she admit right up front that she was Morton Slake's mistress? How did she identify herself?"

"Oh, she just said that her name was Bambi, and she thought I wanted to meet with her. She had plenty of interesting things to tell me."

"I wonder what made her want to talk in the first place."

"At first I thought she just wanted to get even with him somehow."

"But you changed your mind about that?"

"Well—" Marcella hesitated. "How do you know when somebody's really scared, and when they're exaggerating?"

"What do you mean?"

"I mean that she called me up and said she was really scared, but that she had made up her mind and wanted to talk to me. She said that she had an important story to tell."

"Important?"

"That was the word she used. I thought that was interesting. I mean, she may be a bimbo, or she may be a bright woman. I decided that I shouldn't just assume she fit the stereotype."

"Right." Jackie was thinking of some well-known women who did fit the stereotype. They had had their fifteen minutes; some of them even more.

Were there lots of other mistresses of public figures who had more sense, or more discretion? It wasn't fair, as Marcella was suggesting, to assume that Bambi was a bimbo. Just because she had sort of a Playboy Bunny name, and because she was committing adultery with the president of the Palmer city council. And she had decided to get in touch with a well-known investigative reporter, who was doing a profile on the man in question, scheduled for publication four weeks before the election. It was important not to give in to stereotypes.

"Right," said Jackie again, this time more skeptically. She had decided not to give Bambi the benefit of the doubt.

"Well, I was trying to keep an open mind," said Marcella, somewhat defensively. "That's all. I wanted it to be worth my while to spend a Saturday night at the Pancake Palace."

"What else did she say?"

"Not much. Just that she had been thinking things over for the last few weeks, and had decided things were too hot. She had something important to tell me, and she'd feel safer once it was on record."

"Aha."

"That's what *I* thought. Aha! Because, obviously, the people who broke into my apartment and stole my notes figured that I had already talked to Bambi. Or already knew what she was going to tell me."

"Maybe she'll call back and reschedule."

"I doubt it," replied Marcella, sounding resigned. "I think she would have come last night. I just wish I knew what she looked like, or her last name. So I could track her down."

As it turned out, Marcella would soon know what Bambi looked like, and her last name. Unfortunately, it would be too late for Bambi to be interviewed.

CHAPTER 12

It was well past lunchtime when Jackie, Jake, and Peter dropped Isaac off at his house and headed home. Jackie was distracted; she had felt nervous most of the morning, half expecting to see Nate Northcote turn up to watch her boy at play, and to hear Peter's voice calling, "There he is, Ma!" The scenario made her think she might be losing her grip. It was absurd to think that Northcote was some kind of dirty old man, or worse, just because he had asked her an innocent question or two about her dog. Jackie wanted very much to believe in Northcote's innocence.

And she had to admit that she had taken more than just a mild liking to the Palmer prosecuting attorney. If she had been twenty years younger, she might have admitted to having a crush.

In fact, the same sort of adolescent terminology would probably serve now—she certainly wasn't behaving or thinking like a grown-up. She might as well own up to the fact that she was, indeed, snowed. She hadn't had these butterflies in her stomach since long before she'd known Peter's father. She desperately, selfishly, and unreasonably wanted Nate Northcote to turn out to be a good guy, not a creep. "To use the technical term," she muttered aloud.

"What's that, Mom?"

"Nothing, Petey. Just talking to myself."

"Why?"

"Because I'm worried about the man who followed you to Billy Bishop's house yesterday."

"Well, at least he didn't come back today. So I don't think you have to worry anymore."

"I do have to worry. Until I find out who he is and what he wants from you."

Until I make sure it isn't the nice man who took me out to dinner on Friday, she thought bitterly.

But it was one thing to have a crush at seventeen, and quite another to own up to one when you were past the midpoint of your thirties. Or so Jackie reasoned to herself, as she absently melded tuna fish with mayonnaise and bits of onion and celery. When you were thirty-odd, and the mother of a young boy, you could be reasonably supposed to have some distance, some perspective. You could reasonably expect from yourself total self-control, X-ray vision, and an unfailing standard of judgment, uninfluenced by such factors as your own desire for companionship (however slight) or another person's good looks and winning smile.

"Right," said Jackie aloud to Jake. Peter had given up on his mother and gone off, tuna fish sandwich in hand, to have his lunch in the den. She listened for the sound of the TV being switched on, but it didn't come. Peter was probably reading, she thought proudly. Junk books, perhaps, but still books, and that was something in this day and age.

She was deeply grateful that Peter wasn't hooked on video games to the degree that some of his friends were. He could take them or leave them and—in defiance of all the odds—preferred the educational ones to the games. Jackie sometimes thought that the action games offended his sense of reality.

Jackie fixed herself a sandwich, poured out a glass of lemonade, and sat at the kitchen table. As she ate, she talked to Jake, who had the virtue of being an almost perfect listener—especially when there was the promise of a small snack awaiting him at the end of the discourse. He was a dignified dog, but still he was a dog, so while he didn't bother to look at you with pleading eyes, he nonetheless asked the question: *Can I have some too?*

Jackie was deep in her contemplation of Jake's character when the doorbell rang. To her surprise, it was Michael McGowan.

"In time for lunch, as usual," he said with a half-apologetic grin.

"Hi, Michael. Thanks so much for coming by. I thought maybe you were too busy."

"You know I'm never too busy to help out, Jackie. I'm sorry I couldn't come by last night. Something came up."

Jackie allowed herself to wonder briefly who had "come up" for Michael McGowan on Saturday night. Then she put the thought out of her head. As she had been avowing to Marcella, she and Michael were just friends. And, after all, she had been out with Nate Northcote on Friday. Michael had every right to go out on a Saturday if he chose.

"I hardly expect you to be at my beck and call, Michael. I appreciate the fact that you came." Jackie caught the acidity in her tone, and instantly regretted it. Michael McGowan was just getting on her nerves—there was no reason for it, but there it was. She admonished herself to be friendlier. "And you do have perfect timing. Tuna fish. Want a sandwich?"

"Of course. Why do you think I came at lunchtime?" He grinned, and for a moment the old sense of well-being flowed between them. Gone was the clumsy restraint that Jackie had sensed of late.

McGowan seemed to feel the change too, for he transformed his impish grin into a smile of real warmth. "Feels like old times. Me making myself at home in your kitchen. Jake snoring on the floor. You with a delicious tuna fish sandwich at the ready." He smiled winningly as Jackie placed a sandwich, potato chips, and a beer before him.

"You ought to come by more often," suggested Jackie, wiping her hands and sitting down opposite him. Even to her own ears, her voice sounded nervous, falsely casual. What on earth was wrong with her?

He reached down and scratched the snoozing Jake behind the ears. "You agree with that, big guy?"

Jake opened his brown eyes, yawned, and rested his handsome head on his front paws. He knew empty banter when he heard it.

Somehow Jake's presence made Jackie even more acutely aware of the false lightness of her tone. She felt embarrassed; it looked like McGowan did too.

McGowan and Jackie ate their sandwiches in silence for a few moments.

"Well?" asked McGowan at last. "You said you have a problem that I might be able to help you with. Shoot."

Now that he was here, Jackie felt foolish for having called him in the first place. What was there that he could do? She could hardly expect the police to offer round-the-clock protection to an active eleven-year-old. And they weren't on such friendly terms that Jackie could expect McGowan to be her family's protector and guardian. What was more, Jackie's own intuition about the identity of the man in the park made it awkward to discuss. Finally she took a deep breath and plunged ahead with the tale.

"It's not really my story to tell—it's Peter's. But I thought it might be simpler if I were to set out the facts for you. Then you can follow up by asking him whatever questions you want." She repeated, in careful detail, the story that Peter had told her yesterday. McGowan listened carefully, interrupting her from time to time to get specific facts: How far away had the man been sitting? Thirty feet or so, Jackie thought. What newspaper was he reading? No idea. Was there a chance that he had just been expressing casual interest in Jake? Jackie didn't know. Was there a chance that his turning up outside of Billy Bishop's house had been a coincidence? Jackie had no way of knowing that, either.

Jackie answered all of these questions patiently. They were, after all, the same questions that had run through her own mind when she had first heard Peter's tale.

Finally, McGowan sat back and took a thoughtful sip of his beer. He cocked an eyebrow at her. "And you say that neither one of the boys knew the guy. They had no idea who it was."

"No." Jackie knew that her voice contained an edge of something—uncertainty, or perhaps evasiveness. McGowan looked at her sharply but said nothing.

Jackie went on. "My question is this, really: What can I do? Short of telling Peter that he can't go to Isaac's house by himself, that they can't go to the park together without an adult, and so forth." She brushed a strand of dark hair out of her face and looked at McGowan anxiously. "I really had thought it was safe—I mean the place is only around the corner, not two hundred yards from home. And Jake is not exactly the kind of dog that invites strangers to make friends." Jackie glanced down at Jake, whose ears had twitched slightly at the mention of his name.

"For the moment," said McGowan uncomfortably, "I would say no—there's nothing." Despite the pessimism of his words, the detective's voice held a note of calm reassurance for Jackie. There was something in his tone that made Jackie think he would be their guardian and protector.

McGowan looked down at Jake, who had begun to snore rather wheezily. "And you say that Jake didn't notice anything out of the ordinary? Didn't seem worried?"

"Peter didn't seem to think so," replied Jackie. "It's hard to believe anybody would try to befriend him, though. He doesn't look like a mad dog, but he's no golden retriever, either. Not the kind of dog you want to cuddle up with, if you're a stranger to the family."

"Oh, I don't know," protested McGowan. "Jake has never seemed at all threatening to me."

"You're not a stranger, Michael." Jackie blushed slightly as she said this. McGowan had become a stranger, of late. "Besides, you've never really seen him go into his attack mode." Jackie had witnessed this transformation on a few occasions. The first time, it had terrified her into thinking that Jake was a mad dog; more than once he had saved her life—and left her trembling and pale.

She looked down at the half-slumbering dog. It was difficult to believe that he was capable of such ferocity, of such brutal force, but Jackie had seen the metamorphosis with her own eyes; she could attest to the lightning change from a kindly, slightly aged, household dog into ninety pounds of snarling fury. It was a sight to take your breath away.

Jake opened one sleepy eye and regarded his mistress. Then he yawned, shifted his long brown muzzle, and drifted off back to sleep.

McGowan looked from Jake to Jackie and back once more to the dog. Suddenly his face grew somber.

"Listen, Jackie. Cosmo told me that he came by here yesterday and, er, talked to you about things," he said. "About the implications of the Dugan case. And our own involvement in trying to solve it."

Jackie nodded. This was where her thoughts had begun to go too.

"It's an extremely delicate situation," McGowan continued, "and it doesn't look like it's going to get any easier to sort out."

Jackie was suddenly aware of her own anxiety. Michael and Cosmo had warned her long ago that Jake's presence in her household could end up being a dangerous thing. She had thought all of this would blow over—that the police would catch Dugan's killer and put an end to her fears. But now, with the investigation into Dugan's death stalled, and obscured, and full of sinister implications—Jackie was keenly, forcibly reminded of the fact that Jake was the only living witness to the murder of his master.

McGowan went on. "There is absolutely no one we can trust, right now. That's why we asked you to get those lab results for us the other day. It's impossible to know where the stink originates, how many are involved. But there is definitely something rotten going on."

"You've felt that all along, haven't you?"

"Cosmo has. He had to talk me around to seeing his point of view."

"And? Is it getting better or worse for you?"

"The pressure is building. The situation is becoming explosive. We know that for a fact."

"How can you be sure?" asked Jackie. Maybe McGowan and Cosmo were making too much of it. Jackie hated conspiracy theories.

McGowan saw the stubbornness in her eyes, and shook his head regretfully. "I wish we could dodge the whole thing—just get on with our jobs. But there's the small matter of the gun that killed Matt Dugan." Jackie nodded. McGowan continued. "It was stolen from the police property room. The only people who have authorization to be in that room, or to remove anything at all, are the duty sergeant, the captain, and the prosecuting attorney's office."

Jackie's heart sank.

"It bothers me that this stranger in the park was asking questions about Jake. You follow me?"

Jackie nodded, but didn't say a word.

"So. I might as well just come out with it, and you can go ahead and be angry with me. Do you think there's a chance that this guy in the park was Nate Northcote?"

Jackie shook her head. "How would I know, Michael?" Her voice held an edge of irritation, but she wasn't angry with McGowan. Only with herself. "I wasn't there, I only have Peter's and Isaac's description to go on. It could be any relatively tall, dark-haired man."

She knew she sounded defensive, but then, what had she expected? She knew the instant that she picked up the phone to ask Michael to help that she would be exposing her own doubt in Northcote. But that couldn't be helped. Jackie didn't believe it was entirely a coincidence that someone had been asking about Jake, just a day after she'd told Northcote all about him.

And lied, into the bargain.

Jackie and McGowan talked for a while longer, McGowan showing, by an occasional glance at his watch, that he had an appointment of some kind. *Either that,* thought Jackie, *or he's just dying to get out of here, and he feels it's only polite to wait twenty minutes after finishing his lunch.*

But McGowan, despite his clock-watching, didn't seem eager to leave. It had been a long time since they'd had a tête-à-tête, and it was good to catch up over coffee and cookies. Peter appeared from the den, his thumb marking his place in his book, and he and McGowan had a long, serious talk about the incident in Holcomb Park.

When Peter had taken himself off again, Jackie gave way to her curiosity.

"You remember my friend Marcella? The one whose apartment was robbed?"

"Of course," McGowan replied. It wouldn't be easy to forget Marcella, his tone implied.

"Well? Has there been any progress?"

"You mean in her case? The burglary?"

Jackie wondered to herself what other kind of progress McGowan might hope to make with Marcella. She glowered at him. "Of course with the burglary."

"No leads that I know of," said McGowan with a casual shrug, "although I have to admit that it hasn't been at the top of my list to see how the uniforms are following through on that."

"Did Marcella ever call in a further report on it?"

"Don't know." Something in Jackie's thoughtful tone made McGowan curious. "Why?"

"Oh—no reason. Probably not much the police could do, anyway."

"What do you mean?"

"Well—just that after she reported the break-in, she realized that her interviews and notes were stolen for a story she was writing. I had the idea that that might have been the reason for the break-in."

"What kind of story?"

"A profile of Morton Slake."

McGowan was quiet for a long time. Finally, he looked at his watch. "I have to be running, Jackie. I have a homicide on my hands." He rose and reached down to give Jake a parting scratch.

"Wait a second, Michael." Jackie, her curiosity piqued, wasn't at all agreeable to his going without telling her what was happening. She gave him a look, and he sighed.

"Come on, Michael. You have to tell me."

He looked up at her thoughtfully. "I don't want you talking about this, Jackie. Promise me you're not going to rush to the telephone and call Marcella."

"I promise." Obviously, McGowan's story was something good.

"Morton Slake's girlfriend turned up dead last night."

"Bambi?" cried Jackie. "You mean she was murdered?"

McGowan nodded. "Bambi was murdered. Strangled, and left by the side of the interstate. The university exit." McGowan gave Jackie a sharp look. "How on earth do you know about Bambi?"

CHAPTER 13

On Monday morning at nine fifty-six Morton Slake was once more preparing himself for a press conference. This morning, however, he was not his usual composed self.

"How could she do this to me?" he raged. His normally sleek complexion was puffy; his hair stood up over the collar of his suit. Tim Falloes, lint brush in hand, was following Slake around, trying to make him presentable.

"Get away from me with that thing!" Slake bellowed at his would-be valet. Falloes backed away a step or two, watching Slake give way to the spiraling emotions of his temper tantrum.

"That . . . !" With an angry motion, Slake swept his in-box off the desk. It went clattering to the floor, papers flying. He pounded his fist on the desktop, and his little group of paperweights, all scale models of Morton Slake Properties, jumped as though shaken by a miniature earthquake. One of them, the exclusive Slake Towers Condominium, fell over on its side; several little pieces of marble siding fell with a tiny clatter onto the floor.

"I'll see that she pays for this treason." He turned to shake a finger under Falloes's nose. "How dare she? She won't get away with it. I'm going to *ruin* her! She'll be the laughingstock of the city! She'll be a pariah! She'll pay for her treachery, that—"

"Morton! Behave yourself." It was the calm, authoritative voice of Margaret Leaming. She cut through his display of temper like a hot knife through ice cream. "They're waiting for you out front. I suggest that you calm down and let Tim get you ready for the cameras."

Margaret, a look of disgust on her face, turned away and headed for her own small office. Her lips were pursed, and there was a light of resigned conviction in her eyes. She might have been punishing a wayward child. She had been tempted to remind Slake that he had brought his problems on himself.

Morton Slake's difficulty, this Monday morning, was matrimonial.

For the first time since he had begun his mayoral candidacy, he had asked his wife, Marie, to be present with him, to stand next to him and hold his hand at a press conference. He had conjured up a vision of them together, behind the podium and in front of the cameras, displaying Family Values in the Face of Adversity. He envisioned Marie's countenance—beautiful, calm, brave, and restrained—her uplifted eyes proving to the world that her loyalty was unquestioned.

Morton Slake knew that Marie would be with him. She would stand by, in the time-honored fashion of the faithful wife of an adulterous politician whose peccadilloes—hey, nothing more, we all have our little weaknesses—have somehow become a matter of public speculation.

Marie Zug, however, hadn't seen it that way. With a small, satisfied smile on her face, she had politely declined the role. Then she had shut and bolted the front door of the Slake mansion in Morton's face, and given all the servants instructions not to admit him under any circumstances. The servants hated Morton Slake and had been quick to oblige his betrayed wife.

That had happened yesterday evening, after the police had been to see him, and taken him downtown for further questioning in connection with the death of Leslie Wornom, nickname Bambi.

In consequence, Slake hadn't been able to pick up a fresh shirt and a clean suit for this morning's press conference. He'd had to telephone the owner of the Sartorial Shoppe late on Sunday night, and explain matters, and beg for a new suit to be ready for him by ten o'clock Monday morning.

At the Slake mansion, there was much mirth among the servants, and for the first time in years, Marie Zug had a song in her heart.

As he steeled himself to face the cameras alone, Morton Slake tried not to think about the damage he might have done yesterday, when he talked to the police.

The police had been a pain in the neck. For starters, they had come right to his house on Sunday—no telephone call, no warning, nothing. Then they had blurted the whole thing out right in front of Marie, who was standing there in the front hall. McGowan, it was true, had suggested that they talk in private. But how could Slake have known that they had come there about Bambi? He hadn't even known she was dead until they turned up at his house.

And then Marie, hearing the name Bambi, had let out a whoop of laughter.

After which McGowan had persuaded Slake to accompany him downtown, where they could talk in private and wouldn't disturb Mrs. Slake. Marie, on hearing that, had laughed again. "Go right ahead downtown, Morton dear. I won't hold dinner for you."

The questions, once he got downtown, had seemed to go on and on forever. The police had been very nice, very polite. But he had been surprised not to see Max Greenaway there waiting for him. Maybe Max had no idea.

Slake, thinking about the police with a slightly cooler head later on Sunday night (in the Presidential Suite at the Slake Plaza Hotel), had wondered if maybe he had said too much. Well, there was nothing he could do about it now. He should have called a lawyer; he knew that, and the thought that on his own he might have blundered gave him a sinking feeling in the pit of his stomach. But his personal lawyer, the one he trusted, was in Europe. And he had thought it would look worse if he had refused to talk to the police.

Now he had to face the reporters, who had somehow gotten wind of the whole thing. Even his vacationing lawyer had heard about it—he had phoned this morning from the Côte d'Azur to say he'd be home this evening. Probably this evening would be too late for Morton Slake.

He opened the walnut cabinet against a far wall, which concealed a lighted mirror. He smoothed down his hair, allowed Tim Falloes to brush off some imaginary lint, and squared his shoulders. The press were waiting—it was time to take the bull by the horns.

Margaret Leaming gave him a strange look as he passed her desk. Morton Slake shrugged it off. What did he need with Margaret Leaming?

At his desk at the University Precinct, McGowan was going over his notes from yesterday's interview with Slake.

It had just been dumb luck that Leslie Wornom, a.k.a. Bambi, had been a slave to her cellular telephone. Once the police had ID'd the corpse from the driver's license and so forth, it had been a simple matter to find her car, which had been parked outside the Pancake Palace. The telephone was hidden under the driver's seat—not a sound practice, in the view of the police.

From a detective's point of view, cellular phones were a godsend. They were still comparatively rare, and the carriers—for billing purposes—kept meticulous records of every call. Bambi's calls had been extremely easy to trace. There had been at least two every day to the same number, which had turned out to be the private line of Morton Slake, president of the city council and mayoral aspirant. The last call made on the phone had been to that number.

This the Palmer police had discovered within eighteen hours of finding the body. It seemed, to McGowan, to be almost too good to be true. He had, of course, heard the rumors about Slake's infidelity—it was, after all, an election year—but he had never given it much thought, one way or another. Stories like that bored him. But when the girlfriend of a prominent local politician and mayoral hopeful turned up dead—well, that was a different matter altogether.

McGowan had another piece of luck: Evan Stillman was out on three weeks sick leave with a sprained back. Until McGowan had something concrete, therefore, he wouldn't be obliged to tell Stillman about the connection between Slake and the dead woman. He wanted to pursue the lead on his own, without anyone from City Hall running interference for Slake, or telling McGowan to tread softly. McGowan knew what city politics were all about—and he didn't give a damn.

With all this luck running his way, McGowan had left Jackie's house yesterday after lunch, turning up at the Slake house at about four.

Polite, deferential, but firm, he had insisted on talking to Slake; the mayoral aspirant, flushed with success in his morning round of golf, and acting every inch the expansive, welcoming politician, had brought McGowan into the sun porch, where Marie was hand-painting cloth to look like

Indian corn. The fall decorating season would soon be here, she explained with a smile, and with careful handling her faux-corn wreaths would last for a dozen years and more.

It had been a relatively simple matter to get Slake downtown for questioning once the name of Bambi Wornom had been mentioned.

Downtown, during the course of his five-hour interview with Lieutenant McGowan of homicide, Slake had made a surprising admission.

"If I'd known how much trouble mistresses would be," he told the astonished detective, "I never would have bothered."

"Why's that?" McGowan had asked.

"Bambi Wornom wasn't exactly worth all this. Of course, I'm sorry she got herself killed, and all that. But look what's happening to me."

"What exactly is happening to you, Mr. Slake?"

"Well, do you suppose I'll be able to keep any of this from the press?"

"No. Does that bother you?"

Slake rolled his eyes. "Of course it bothers me." Slake spoke slowly, precisely, as though explaining some very basic principle to a half-wit. "I'm running for mayor. Mayors are supposed to be—well, they're not supposed to have a girlfriend who gets herself killed and dumped on the highway. The press will have a field day."

"If I were you," advised McGowan, "I wouldn't let it bother you. It's only August, after all. You have two months plus till the election. Probably this'll blow over."

Then McGowan had sat back and allowed Morton Slake to go on, with an even more astonishing series of admissions. He had no alibi for Saturday at nine-thirty—the approximate time of death, as established by the coroner's office. He hadn't really been getting along very well with

Bambi, and lately he had been thinking of putting an end to their relationship anyway. No, he didn't think there was anyone else who knew about her, except for Tim Falloes, his administrative aide.

Nobody else? McGowan had pushed.

Well, Margaret, of course. Margaret Leaming was his secretary, and she knew everything about him. She disapproved of Bambi, so they never discussed her, but Slake knew that Margaret knew.

But as far as Morton Slake could figure, they were the only two who could possibly have known about the connection between himself and Bambi.

Thus it was that on Monday morning, while Morton Slake was facing the avid curiosity of the press, Michael McGowan made himself comfortable in a chair in Margaret Leaming's office. He had a few very brief questions to ask her, he said. He hoped that she wouldn't mind.

CHAPTER 14

The soft music playing in the background ought to have soothed Jackie's nerves, but she was as jumpy as a cat. She took a sip of her drink and did her best to smile.

Nate Northcote, looking casual and handsome, grinned at her from across the table. He reached out idly for her hand.

"So when do I get to meet this fabulous son of yours? And Jake the Wonder Dog?"

"Peter's gone off fishing with his father," said Jackie, resisting the impulse to draw her hand away. She had to be casual, casual. She was scared to death. "So I guess our little outing will have to wait."

Cooper had called yesterday, right after McGowan had left, to invite Peter fishing for a few days. Jackie had leapt at the chance to get her boy away to the middle of some mountain lake, where there were no strange men watching him in the twilight. She had even talked Cooper into inviting Isaac along. Three men in a tub, Cooper had remarked, laughing. His old fishing boat wasn't elegant, but it was safe. *Safer, right now, than Isabella Lane and Holcomb Park*, thought Jackie. "He'll be gone all week, maybe longer."

"Well, I suppose that's too bad." Northcote's grin was a

knowing one. "I guess you'll be at loose ends?"

Jackie smiled thinly. "Yes and no. School starts up again in less than three weeks. I have a ton of planning to do, and it will be a relief to have some time to myself. It's a rare luxury for the mother of an eleven-year-old."

"Did Peter take the dog along on his little adventure?"

"No." Jackie's answer had too much firmness to it. "That is, Isaac has three dogs. Peter's best friend. They decided to take some of his—he's got two that like to swim. Ours isn't really a very recreational dog."

"Not the kind to play endless hours of fetch?"

"Hardly." Jackie's blood ran cold. This couldn't all be a coincidence?

"You seem distracted. You all right?"

"Sorry, Nate. Yes, I'm fine."

"I don't mean to push you about meeting your boy, you know. I hope I haven't been coming on too strong. We'll talk about something else. Impersonal." He smiled engagingly. "Did you hear that Morton Slake is considering dropping out of the race?"

Jackie nodded. "That whole situation is pretty peculiar, if you ask me. I mean—of *course* he should drop out. Don't you think?"

Bambi Wornom's demise had been front-page news all day. Well, it wasn't so much the loss of Bambi as the discovery that she was Slake's mistress that had set Palmer on its ear. Marie Zug, after all, was their very own folk heroine. Any treason against Marie was treason against the heart and soul of Palmer.

What was more, one of the newspapers (not the *Chronicle*) had dug up some early photos of Bambi, from the days when she thought she might like to be an actress. Probably, thought Jackie, when she saw the photos, some man had told her she had the body for it. The photos were average, as such things go, but Bambi was a sensation—in death, as never in life.

Bambi's body had been found by a passing motorist at about ten-fifteen on Saturday night. She had been dead only a short time, an hour or less. Her murderer had evidently dumped her from a car that was proceeding up the university exit ramp of the interstate. The rain and the fog had made visibility limited, and so far there were no witnesses.

"It is strange. More going on than meets the eye." The waiter arrived with their appetizers. Northcote had ordered smoked trout; Jackie was having oysters from the Chesapeake Bay. They dug in, and in a moment Jackie began to feel better. Northcote went on. "But anyway, Slake had better forget about the election. He won't have time. He's got a lot of things to sort out—I heard through the grapevine that Marie has locked him out of the house."

"Uh-oh."

"Uh-oh is right. Plus—did you know that the seed money for Slake Properties was all hers?"

"No kidding!"

"No kidding. So if they divorce, Slake is looking at being on the receiving end, alimony-wise. More than three fourths of his properties are actually in her name."

"Aha!"

"Aha what?"

Jackie bit her tongue. She had heard earlier from Marcella, who had talked to McGowan, that Marie Zug was apparently taking the whole business in a cheery fashion. "Aha, nothing," she said. "Only that I always had a hard time believing in him as a dynamic captain of industry, or whatever."

"I would say dynamic's not really the word for him." Northcote studied Jackie closely. "What *were* you doing in his office that day?"

Jackie opened her eyes wide and reached for an oyster. She dipped it carefully in mignonette sauce, then paused. "I was snooping around. Just for the hell of it."

"I thought so." Northcote eyed her narrowly. "I didn't believe that story about documentary filmmaking, you know."

"No? But the seniors *are* making a documentary on the municipal government."

"Yes, they are. With Fred Jackson, the senior adviser and the director of the summer school. You aren't teaching in the summer school. And even if you were, you teach film history to freshmen and sophomores. Not documentary filmmaking to seniors."

Jackie gave him a blank look. He took a bite of his smoked trout and regarded her calmly. "I've been doing some checking up on you. I have resources, you know."

She suddenly felt terribly spooked. Why was Nate Northcote checking up on her? Because he liked her? Or because he had caught her in Morton Slake's office, talking on the phone to Bambi? Bambi, who was now dead, strangled, not able to talk anymore, to Marcella Jacobs or to Jackie or to anyone.

The police had found Bambi's car parked outside of a restaurant more than two miles away from where the body had been dumped. Jackie shivered. Here they were at Suki's Place—which was evidently Northcote's usual haunt—and Jackie figured they were just about two miles from the university exit of the interstate. Jackie wished that she had remembered to ask Michael which restaurant. Was Bambi's car found at the Pancake Palace, where Marcella had gone to meet her? Or was it some other restaurant?

Suddenly, looking at Nate across the table as though he were the very devil incarnate, Jackie felt a rush of determination. She was tired of having her perfectly nice evenings spoiled by a groundless aura of suspicion. If Michael McGowan didn't know whom he could rely on, at least Jackie would find out for herself. This atmosphere of mistrust was all wrong. It was unbalanced, unhealthy. You ought to be able to tell who your friends were.

Jackie regarded Nate carefully, and steeled herself. One way or another, she would find out.

She smiled at Nate as the waiter approached with their entrees.

"You seem to be taking a kind of ghoulish pleasure in the whole case," Jackie remarked. "It may get awkward for you if the police find out that Morton Slake killed his mistress."

"Why would that be awkward for me?"

"Oh, I don't know. I kind of figured you guys were friends."

"Nope. I can't stand him, if you want to know the truth."

"Oh." Jackie gave him another look. What had he been doing in Slake's office that day?

"So now you want to know what I was doing in his office that day?" he asked with a friendly smirk.

"Well, it's really none of my business—"

"No, but that's immaterial. I was only looking for Margaret."

"The secretary."

"Come, come, Jackie. I'm surprised at you. Aren't you an enlightened woman of the twentieth century?"

"Well, of course I am," said Jackie with a small frown. What had she said that was so unenlightened?

"Then you ought to know better than to dismiss someone like Margaret Leaming as 'the secretary.' " He scowled at her. "Really, I'm surprised at you."

"I didn't mean anything pejorative by it. And I certainly think it's dumb to say 'administrative assistant' when you mean 'secretary.' The position of secretary is a very demanding, difficult one, requiring intelligence, competence, a passion for neatness, and a willingness to let all the credit for your hard work go to someone else. So why *not* say 'secretary'?"

This argument was familiar ground for Jackie, who hated the euphemisms of modern life. Human resources specialists, sanitation engineers, administrative assistants—what was wrong with describing things as they actually were? But there was an epidemic of euphemism in their culture, in this century.

"Secretary," said Jackie stubbornly. "You're the one who thinks I'm saying 'just a secretary.' "

Northcote laughed, long and hard, his eyes filling with tears of mirth. "Well!" he exclaimed, catching his breath. "I certainly pushed one of your buttons, didn't I?"

Jackie smiled and nodded. "Why were you looking for Margaret?" Jackie knew the question sounded intrusive. Northcote gave her a funny look.

"I needed to check Slake's calendar. We sometimes have to meet on a professional basis. Meetings, meetings, and more meetings." His voice had a bored tone, which Jackie suspected wasn't real. People generally love to tell other people that they've been to meetings, and the vaguer the better. Meetings sound important—all these busy people have rushed away from their desks to be in each other's presence.

"The price of a high-profile job in the public service," said Jackie teasingly.

"When the mayor summons us," Northcote said with a grin, "we polish our shoes and scurry off to see him."

"Like the Wizard of Oz," Jackie suggested, regaining the lightness in her tone.

"Exactly. Egg-zackly, as my nephew says. That's how we

pass the day away, in the merry old City Hall. Crimebusters and civic leaders, hand in hand, doing the right thing for John Q. Public. Killers and burglars and thieves, oh, my!"

Jackie laughed. "Well, I think you're making progress, anyway. The gun-control bill was passed. Did you get the inside story on why Slake changed his position on it?"

"No. He wouldn't talk about it." Northcote shook his head. "I don't mind telling you that I was really shocked. And, to tell the truth, I was pretty angry about it."

"Why? Weren't you supporting it?"

"Of course, my dear." He gave her a goofy grin. "It's just that he wasted so damn much of everybody's time. We'd spent months and months lobbying for that bill, and he'd been incredibly stubborn about giving our people time in the council debates, and so forth. Then he does a one-eighty on us and pretends like it's been his bill, his baby, all along. Called the newspapers and told them he'd rammed it through the reluctant council. I could have killed him, I was so angry."

"But instead you shook hands." Jackie hadn't failed to notice the photo, carried by the *Chronicle* on the day after the council vote. Max Greenaway, Nate Northcote, and Morton Slake, all grinning at each other, while the mayor, obliged to go along with it, signed the bill into law.

Greenaway, Northcote, and Slake, it occurred to Jackie, were an unlikely threesome if ever there was one.

"Yeah," said Northcote. "And Max got stuck inviting Slake to his party. Thought it would absolve him from any further obligations to the man. Those were his exact words."

Jackie thought back to the scene at Max Greenaway's house last Friday night. She had thought then that Slake's presence had struck a discordant note—the more so as Jane Bellamy, his rival in the mayoral race, was also there. And also, clearly, a close friend of the police commissioner's.

"It probably does absolve him," said Jackie. That party had been a dream for someone like Slake. All the money in the world wouldn't get him on another party list like that. Of course, being mayor of Palmer would have. Or maybe not. People in Palmer tended not to be overly impressed by politicians.

"Probably," agreed Northcote with a smile. "Now Greenaway just owes the rest of us, for inviting us to a party with Morton Slake."

CHAPTER 15

"I suppose I may appear either hard-hearted or stupid?"

Michael McGowan shifted uneasily in his chair at the kitchen table. In a way, he relished moments like this, but Marie Zug was proving to be not quite what he had expected.

"Is that what you think, Captain?"

"Lieutenant, ma'am."

"Lieutenant." Marie Zug waved the distinction away and bent her head over the kitchen table. "You don't mind if I work while we chat, do you?" With a small sponge soaked in gold paint, she was stamping out some kind of a pattern on the un-shiny side of a huge roll of white freezer paper. McGowan, who didn't have any feeling at all for arts and crafts, averted his eyes from what seemed to him a lunatic pursuit.

Marie Zug had apologized to McGowan, on his arrival, for the state of the kitchen, and he had to agree that it looked like the touch-down point of a particularly vicious cyclone. There were bits and pieces of gingham everywhere, scraps of cotton, wicker baskets of every size, jars of dye, ceramic jars in various stages of being painted, and all the other odds and ends of Marie Zug's calling.

She had explained to McGowan that her helpers had all

gone off somewhere—gathering pinecones, or something, as far as McGowan could tell. Her helpers sounded more like chipmunks than employees, he thought, but he was just as glad there were no helpers around. He welcomed the chance to see Marie Zug alone. Later on he would tackle Bambi Wornom's colleagues.

"As you know, Ms. Zug, I don't mean to intrude, and I can see you're busy. But I did want to ask you one or two questions about the late Ms. Wornom. I understand that she worked for you as a"—he consulted a notebook—"bow specialist. That right?"

"Bow stylist, Captain. Yes, that's correct. She worked for me for three years, and whatever I know about her—or *thought* I knew about her—I will gladly tell you." She brushed back a lock of her blond hair with the back of her hand, and gave McGowan a conspirator's smile. "Please, don't apologize for doing your job, you're welcome to ask. You might not like what you hear from me, that's the only thing. I tend to speak my mind. So far, I have found it works for me. Other people are different, but it works for me." She stopped for breath.

So McGowan began by asking questions, but he soon found it was not really necessary. Marie Zug needed no prodding; all she required was an audience. McGowan had the feeling that she would have poured forth exactly the same monologue for a taxi driver, or the Portuguese ambassador, or Elizabeth Taylor. Nonetheless, it seemed to him that Marie Zug was strangely remote in her assessment of the young woman. McGowan strained to hear a touch of bitterness, but he could detect none. He found that odd; Marie Zug seemed to anticipate him in this matter, however, as she had in every other since the interview began.

"But anyway, just let me finish this one thought. Maybe

I *am* silly. Definitely not hard-hearted. Could anyone who loves beautiful things as much as I do be *hard* on the inside? No. But maybe I am foolish. The thing is, I have been wanting to divorce Morton for years. Well, just one look at the two of us should tell you why, Captain. We are very different people. He has no feeling for beautiful things, none at all." She shook her head. Such a pitiful lack. "But I just never got around to it. Well, I was busy, as you can see." She nodded vaguely to the gilt-flecked freezer paper on the table before her. "And everyone says that divorce can be very disruptive. I didn't want to have to think about two things at once—I wanted to concentrate on my business."

"I see." McGowan felt helpless in the face of this stream of blather. He was drowning in her noise, but there seemed to be no way to stop it. Either the woman was trying to put one over on him, or she was totally out of touch. Probably only her therapist knew for sure.

"So." She came to the end of a long row of gilt blobs and adjusted the freezer paper slightly. She tilted her head, like a robin listening for a worm, and examined her handiwork. She found it good. McGowan enjoyed the brief respite.

She began on another row, and took up her narration again, preceding it with a wise smile.

"Then, of course, he decided to run for mayor. Well, I thought, I've put up with him this long, and there's nobody else in my life, there's just my work, and he doesn't interfere with that. So if he leaves me alone and behaves himself I'll wait till after the election to divorce him. He's such a dreadful little creep. When he was younger, he wasn't so bad, and I thought I could do something with him. That, of course, was just the vanity of youth. But I really did think I could do something with him."

Like she was doing something with freezer paper, thought McGowan. He nodded sympathetically. Maybe she had a knack for that kind of thing, but Morton Slake—unlike freezer paper and pinecones—resisted improvement.

"You had no idea about his, er, affair with Miss Wornom, then?"

"Of course not. You don't think I would have kept her on as a helper if I'd known? I mean, she was welcome to him, in a way, but not until after the divorce. She should have known better. She should have waited." Marie Zug adjusted the freezer paper again. "After all, she knew perfectly well I'd be dumping him in the spring."

"She knew?" This was an interesting angle.

"Well, of course she knew. My helpers aren't just employees, you know. We work very hard together, and there's a kind of spiritual connection that binds us, through our creativity, to each other."

"I see."

"If you want my thoughts on the subject, I would say that Bambi hadn't realized before what a little creep Morton is. So she took up with him, and then she found out. Poor thing." Marie Zug honestly sounded sorry for the girl. "Well, she probably made the same mistake everyone around him makes—she probably thought he was rich and successful. He's not. I'm the rich one, and if you are interested in finding out where Morton's success comes from, I'd suggest you talk to Margaret Leaming. Morton couldn't wipe his nose without her there to tell him where it is."

McGowan nodded. "So I've heard," said the detective.

This was the same picture he'd gotten from Greenaway and the mayor, both of whom had called him in for long consultations on the case. At least in her assessments of her husband's talent—or lack of it—Marie Zug seemed to be on the ball. Maybe there was a grain of truth among the chaff.

"But, of *course,* little Bambi was right about one thing. She thought he'd be mayor, which of course he would have. Hah. Too late now." Marie Zug stamped emphatically at the freezer paper with her gold-dipped sponge. She held up a corner of the paper for McGowan to see. "You like?"

"Yes, ma'am."

She chuckled. "It must have sounded pretty tempting. That is, if Morton could tempt you in the first place. At least, when he tempted me, he was young and fit and had his own hair." She looked sharply at McGowan. "You did know, didn't you, that it's a wig?"

"Uh, no, actually." McGowan made a hasty note, and Marie Zug continued.

"Of course, she had sort of scraped herself up from nowhere, she was totally self-taught, and she had no family. At least, no parents or brothers or sisters. They were all killed in a tornado down in Texas when she was a little thing, and she was adopted by some people somewhere. Philadelphia, maybe. But they're dead too."

McGowan suddenly felt a pang of pity for the dead girl. She must have been a pretty little thing, when she came up to Palmer as an orphan.

"If you were a Freudian, Captain," said Marie, pronouncing it "Froodian," "then you might think that she was looking for a family, that's why she adopted us. First me. Before she came to Palmer she worked in some of those casinos in Atlantic City. But she told me she got fed up with the kind of people there, and saw that there really wasn't a future in that kind of work. Besides, she felt pretty strongly that she ought to be involved with art, somehow. She was quite a talented little thing."

"Was she?"

"She could make a piece of ribbon do all kinds of things, and she had the greatest ideas about using dried seed pods in decorative ways."

McGowan was surprised. These talents were at odds with the little gold-digger he had privately imagined Bambi to be.

"So, anyway," Marie Zug went on, "she moved to Palmer and took a vocational course at the Downtown Arts School. Then somehow she heard about me, and she just talked her way in the door, like some kind of salesman. I think that to her my little studio must have seemed like a cozy, busy nest. I was her mother, and all the other little nestlings were here with us."

Marie Zug lifted her head from the freezer paper to look McGowan in the eye. "And then maybe I betrayed her somehow, not by dying, which is how the rest of her families betrayed her, but I did something that made her not love me anymore. For the life of me, I can't think what it might have been. But she climbed in the sack with my husband, to pay me back."

She bent her head over the freezer paper once more. "If I believed in the Froodian interpretation, Captain, that's maybe where I'd start. To find out what she wanted with Morton in the first place. You'd better first find out how I done her wrong."

At eight o'clock that evening, at the Juniper Tavern, Michael McGowan was having a cheeseburger and a well-deserved beer. He was in his usual booth at the back, and Rachel Gibson, the waitress, was hovering nearby to bring reinforcements as soon as they were needed. Across the table, Cosmo Gordon was amused. He was listening to the tale of McGowan's visit to Marie Zug.

"I just kind of pushed a switch somewhere, I think,"

McGowan said. "I turned it on and I couldn't get it to turn off. Reminded me of a faucet I had once, in my kitchen. You couldn't ever get the cold water to stop, unless you used pliers." He took an enormous bite of his cheeseburger. "Marie Zug. She was just like that faucet. Unstoppable. She sat there, plonking down gold paint and talking."

"Think she's crazy?"

"I don't know." McGowan grinned and dipped a french fry in ketchup. "She's made ten or twelve million dollars in the last five years from her little cottage industry. Definitely got her head screwed on where money's concerned."

"Maybe she's just jealous. Of Bambi, I mean."

McGowan considered this. "Hard to say," he commented at last. "She says, of course, that she was going to divorce Morton, but that's what they always say, the ones who murder their husbands' girlfriends. They think it makes them less suspicious."

Gordon chuckled, polished off his beer, and signaled to Rachel that it was time for another round. "Isn't it amazing? They do always say it."

"The thing is, I think maybe I believe this one."

"Do you?"

"Well—I wouldn't want her as an eyewitness in a case. But she's one of those real stream-of-consciousness talkers. I don't think she's capable of guiding her conversation in any way. Like some kind of nervous condition prevents her from realizing that somebody else might have a word or two to say."

"Sounds like great company at a dinner party."

"Whew!" agreed McGowan. "If Slake does win the mayoral race, she'll be a real civic burden for people like Max Greenaway."

"Yeah. Except old Max won't have to put up with it. Slake will appoint someone new."

The two men regarded each other for a moment. "Let's not talk about that," Gordon said finally.

"About Commissioner Stillman?" McGowan's voice contained an unusually bitter note. "No, let's not think about it. Maybe Slake will lose."

"Maybe." Gordon reached over and took a french fry from McGowan's plate. "But tell me more about the wife. You think she was telling the truth?"

"Put it this way: I don't think she's enough in control to hide it if she murdered Bambi."

"Hmm."

"Anyway, I'll need your sympathy. I have to go back again."

"Ye gods. What for?"

"I'd like to get more information out of her."

"Such as?"

"Such as why her husband decided to vote for the gun-control bill."

Gordon scratched a cheek thoughtfully. "That was kind of a sudden turnabout, wasn't it?"

"I'd be interested to know where the pressure came from."

"You think it was a bribe?"

"Come on, Cosmo. You know that nobody backing the gun-control bill has any money for lobbying. That's all on the other side of the issue."

Cosmo Gordon nodded his head in agreement. This was a problem that they had faced for a long time in trying to get the bill through the city council. "Maybe he just had a change of heart."

"Maybe. Or maybe Margaret Leaming told him it was a smart move to make."

"Who's Margaret Leaming? The Good Witch of the North?"

"No—more like his fairy godmother. She's the one who makes everything possible for him."

"Including getting rid of cumbersome girlfriends?"

"According to Marie, she wipes his nose for him every morning."

CHAPTER 16

In the prettily renovated apartment on Cider Lane, with its high ceilings and polished parquet floors and elaborate moldings, Jackie and Marcella were having a field day. The two friends were slouched on Marcella's sofa, drinking diet colas and polishing off the nubs at the bottom of an enormous bowlful of popcorn. Jake, having partaken of the feast, was asleep on a corner of a rose-and-blue Persian rug, which looked very much to Jackie like it might be the real thing. Reporters evidently did pretty well for themselves these days, she thought.

Peter and Isaac were still off on their fishing trip with Cooper, and Jackie had had two days of hedonistic bliss. Last night's dinner with Nate Northcote had ended pleasurably enough, although Jackie was still on the fence about him. Probably she was reading too much into all of his questions about Peter and Jake, but she still found his inquisitiveness somewhat unnerving. The evening had ended without her making up her mind, one way or another, about him. Except that he was amusing, probably rich (dinner at Suki's twice!), and very good-looking.

Tonight, she and Marcella had experienced a near-perfect evening. They had conscientiously consumed a leafy, fresh salad for dinner. This they had followed up with a huge bowl of popcorn (with real butter, *not* "butter flavor"), endless diet sodas, and a rented movie. Life didn't get much better than this. In terms of perfect lying-around-on-the-sofa enjoyment, there were few movies, in Jackie's book, that could rival *The Big Easy*. It had just ended, leaving the women momentarily at a loss for words. They were still enjoying the effects of the last few scenes.

"The truly great thing about that movie," said Jackie at last, speculative, "is Ellen Barkin. Is there a woman who doesn't identify with her?"

Marcella shook her head. "No. She's great, I'll admit. She's Everywoman. But the *great* thing, the absolutely truly great thing, is Dennis Quaid. Everything else follows from that. Remember when he says, 'Your luck is about to change, *chère*'?"

The women lapsed into silence, remembering. It was a remarkable moment, no doubt about it.

"Ellen Barkin only becomes great," continued Marcella, "because she gets Dennis Quaid and brings out the good in him. And we as filmgoers can be satisfied because we know deep down that she deserves him."

"We know, deep down, that *we* deserve him, you mean. And we are really and truly like Ellen Barkin—brilliant, shy, a little uncertain, but highly principled. So that, by the commutative principle, we are the ones who actually get him. In effect, it is *our* luck that is about to change, *chère*."

"Right. Thank you, Professor," said Marcella.

"Plus, they get married, instead of just kissing at the end, which is so square that it's totally cool."

"A happy ending."

They thought about this. Both of them knew from experience just how long happy endings were likely to endure. The problems always arose after the final frame.

"A happy ending is really just a point in a continuum of good and bad things that happen to you," said Marcella.

"Thank *you*, Professor," said Jackie.

Neither woman, however, was the kind to give up on the idea of more or less permanent happiness, just because she hadn't quite found it.

"I think you can have *prevailing* happiness in your life," said Jackie.

"What's that? Some weather condition, like a prevailing westerly?"

"Yeah." Jackie thought about it. "Right. The climate of your life."

"Now she's a meteorologist," Marcella remarked to Jake, who had begun to snore. "Your dog snores, Jackie."

"I know. Prevailing happiness all depends on your outlook."

"Said Pollyanna."

"It does."

"It depends on who you meet," contradicted Marcella. "You can try to let happiness prevail all you want, but if you only meet creeps and losers, you're never going to end up like Ellen Barkin."

Jackie shook her head. They had been over this ground before. "Who you meet is also totally dependent on your outlook. Your outlook determines what you see when you look at the world, and therefore who you meet."

They thought some more.

"So?" asked Marcella finally. "What about him?"

"Who?" replied Jackie evasively.

"Don't give me that." Marcella rose and went to the kitchen for more sodas and ice. Jackie heard the freezer door open. "Want a frozen Snickers bar?" Marcella called to Jackie.

"God, no," said Jackie with a laugh. "Not for at least half an hour."

Marcella came back in with the drinks. "Okay, I've given you time to collect your thoughts. So tell me." She put the drinks down on the coffee table and went to a wooden cabinet in one corner. Inside was the new stereo she had bought to replace the stolen one. "Did you check it out?" asked Marcella, selecting an old James Taylor album for the turntable. "It's even got a CD player in it."

"God, you're equipped," said Jackie with a laugh.

"Yeah, all I need is some CDs," smirked Marcella. She put down the needle, and James Taylor's voice came up, reedy but soothing and familiar, saying that he was your handyman.

"I need a handyman," said Marcella, slouching once more on the sofa. "Okay. Now. Tell me."

"I feel kind of like Ellen Barkin," replied Jackie, a glint of humor in her eyes.

"Right."

"I *do*. See, the thing is that the people I know who are connected to the police—"

"You mean your other boyfriend."

"Yikes! Let me finish," said Jackie, annoyed. Just once she would like to have a conversation without somebody telling her that Michael McGowan was her boyfriend. She wasn't even sure they were friends anymore. "My other friends on the force don't seem to think very highly of him. But I try and try to figure out what's wrong with him, and he just seems like a perfectly nice guy to me."

"Want my opinion?"

Jackie looked at Marcella warily. "Sure."

"He's too handsome. Men who are that handsome always bear a deep scar on their psyches."

"Not always," protested Jackie. "Look at Dennis Quaid."

"That was a *movie*." Marcella rolled her eyes and flopped back against an arm of the sofa.

"Yeah," admitted Jackie, "but it was a really convincing movie."

"So now all you have to do is find out if he's a crook or not. What's he suspected of, anyway?"

"Oh, I'm not really sure," lied Jackie. There was no way she'd spill the beans to Marcella. The ace reporter would be on the story like a shot, exposing a hint of corruption and wrongdoing, and all the other members of the press would take up the hunt. Before you could say "Serpico," Michael and Cosmo would be out of a job or maybe—if their ideas were true—they would be just as dead as Matt Dugan. "It's not so much that he's suspected of anything in particular. I think they just don't like him."

"Well," pointed out Marcella, in the tone of one being utterly reasonable, "you could hardly expect them to like him. After all, he stole you away from Michael."

"Oh, for heaven's sake!" yelled Jackie. Jake awoke with a start, checking quickly to be sure all was well. He rested his head on his paws, but kept a watchful eye on Marcella.

"Look. You woke up your watchdog."

"Sorry, Jake," said Jackie. Then she glared at her friend. "Would you lay off about Michael? I *told* you—he's just not interested in me."

"Okay, okay." Marcella was silent for a moment, stifling a laugh. She had always enjoyed getting a rise out of Jackie. "You know, I had a long interview with him about Bambi."

"I figured. I hope you don't mind that I told him about your appointment with her."

"No, not at all. I mean, now that she's dead, what difference would it make?"

"What do you think happened?"

"I think Morton Slake's crazy wife killed her."

"You do?" Jackie sat up, interested. "Wait. Why do you say that Marie is crazy?"

"She spends her life tying bows and dyeing pinecones. She's *got* to be crazy. Only crazy people are content with a lifetime of occupational therapy."

"No, Marcella. You're being too hard on her. I think she's sort of a genius. I mean—it takes a lot of imagination to make the whole of America yearn for your faux Indian corn door wreaths."

"Not quite the whole of America," said Marcella stubbornly.

"Well, I wasn't including *us*." Jackie giggled. "Although if I had to entertain a houseful of Cooper's boring business friends, I would *definitely* use her cheese-puff recipe. That's the only language some people understand."

"Then you could have put a sign on your front door. 'Kingswood Spoken Here.' "

The two friends giggled.

"Really," said Jackie at last, "do you think Marie killed Bambi?"

"Did you know that Bambi's real name is Leslie Wornom?" countered Marcella.

"Yes," replied Jackie somberly, reaching for the popcorn. "I saw it in the paper."

"No wonder she didn't mind being called Bambi."

"I agree," said Jackie. "But now that she's dead, Marcella, how are we going to get your Slake scoop?"

That was, after all, the final question confronting the women tonight. They had resolved most of the other important issues facing them—dinner, Snickers bars, Dennis Quaid and Ellen Barkin, and prevailing happiness. They had decided to leave Nate Northcote up in the air awhile longer. The only thing they still had to do was to solve the murder of Bambi Wornom.

Marcella, having gotten over the disappointment of missing out on the Bambi interview, had been trying to come up with another way to get at the truth about Slake. By now both women—and most of Palmer—were convinced that he was hiding something.

Of course, the revelations about Bambi—everything from her name to her occupation to her dimensions—had set up a mildly manic preoccupation in town. But Marcella was persuaded that Bambi would have been a mere conduit, had she lived to tell her tale. The secret about Morton Slake hadn't died with the curvy blonde from Texas.

"I think the whole thing has something to do with drug money," Marcella said at last. "I don't think you go around murdering people just because they're somebody's girlfriend."

"No," mused Jackie, "but there's no evidence at all that Morton Slake has connections in the drug underworld. Whereas he *does* have connections in the construction industry." The stereotypical image of a black-shirted mobster with wide lapels flitted briefly through Jackie's mind. "Cement shoes and all that."

"But Bambi was strangled," pointed out Marcella reasonably. "Mobsters always use some special way of killing people. They don't just strangle them and dump them on the road."

"No, I guess not," said Jackie. "She must have known something. Don't you think?"

"Of course. That was going to be my whole story." Marcella frowned. "You know, before Bambi turned up dead—and turned out to be who she turned out to be—I was the only person in the whole city who even bothered to look at Slake. Now look what's happened. No reporter can get near him. Him or his crazy wife."

"Really? Why don't you go in disguise?"

"It won't work. They know me already—Slake and Marie, both. I've been to the house about ten times."

"Too bad that you didn't meet Bambi on one of those visits."

"You're telling me." Marcella shook her head. "Although I don't know if she would have been ready to talk then. I think something happened. She got fed up, or scared. Otherwise, she never would have called me."

"No sign of your notes, is there?" asked Jackie meaningfully.

"None." Marcella sounded discouraged. "Not that there would be any use for a story like that anymore. My editor killed it anyway. Now I've got to cover the voting on the municipal financing bonds for the new shopping center out by the interstate."

"God, how dull."

"You're telling me! They really ought to put me back on the crime beat. At least so I can cover Bambi."

"Will they?"

"Only if I come up with the story first. And now I have all this competition. What a drag."

Jackie agreed that it was a drag. The two women talked some more about possible angles, and then Jackie and Jake departed.

During their conversation, Jackie had come up with an idea. But she wasn't sure it would work, so she kept it to herself, and decided to go home and think it over. She glanced at her watch. It was only nine-thirty, but she felt exhausted. The price of living the life of Riley.

She emerged into the muggy August air. The thunderstorm that had threatened earlier had never materialized; gone, along with the threat, was any promise of fresh night air. In place of rain, a heavy, dank mist was settling in. Jackie put her yellow slicker over her arm and looked up and down Cider Lane. The little street was poorly lighted and looked oddly menacing through the refracting lens of the fog.

Jackie stood a moment at the top of Marcella's stoop. She couldn't see much more than a few yards in front of her. Tensing, she wound Jake's lead around her fist several times, pulling the dog in closer to her, and set off down the stairs to the street.

The area surrounding the university wasn't the safest neighborhood even under the best conditions; tonight, it was positively spooky. Glancing toward Chestnut Street, Jackie could see that there was very little traffic—the area around school was always deserted this time of the summer. Nor did there seem to be any other pedestrians in the narrow little cobblestoned lane.

Jackie decided that she was letting things get to her. She bit her lower lip and walked on, determined not to slacken her pace.

A shadow detached itself from the wall as Jackie passed and silently fell into step behind her.

CHAPTER 17

Jackie kept walking, her grip on Jake's lead tightening. Her breath came in short gasps; the air felt thick and heavy, as though she could not breathe for the fog.

In a moment she heard the unmistakable sound of a footstep behind her.

Jake was alive at once, transformed. He bared his teeth and let out a low growl. Jackie spun around, in time to see a tall figure lift a hand to strike her.

"Get him, Jake," Jackie commanded.

Jake leapt viciously through the air, but he was not in time. A heavy blow crashed down on Jackie's head, and all was blackness.

McGowan and Gordon were finished drinking and eating for the evening. They had talked over every angle of the "Dear Slaying" (as Bambi's murder had been tastelessly referred to in one of the tabloids), and had moved on for a thorough dissection of Jackie's relationship with Nate Northcote. Without some kind of evidence of malfeasance, McGowan had urged, they really were not entitled to butt in. Gordon, in a departure from his usual laissez-faire attitude about other people's lives, didn't agree. He was worried about Jackie's well-being.

The two old friends argued happily for half an hour or
so, as though there were anything they could do about it
if Jackie were to fall in love with Northcote. McGowan
had the idea that Gordon knew more about the prosecuting
attorney's private life than he deemed it prudent to tell.
But there was no sense going digging for complexities in
the issue. Michael McGowan, faced with the facts, realized
that he was just plain jealous.

But there was not much he could do about that—not
tonight, at any rate. He glanced at his watch. McGowan
was hoping to talk briefly again with Marcella Jacobs,
the reporter whom Bambi had been planning to meet at the
Pancake Palace on Saturday night. McGowan had taken
Marcella's statement on Sunday, but since then a few more
questions had presented themselves. It was time he went
back for more.

McGowan, having the idea that all reporters burned the
midnight oil, went to the phone and dialed the *Chronicle*.
Marcella was long gone; it was nearly nine-thirty. She'd be
home, if she was going home, and Cider Lane was right on
his way. He said good night to Cosmo and headed through
the gathering summer fog across the Rodgers University
campus.

Jackie didn't exactly know when she'd felt more foolish.
As she swam back to consciousness on the sidewalk in
front of Marcella's house, she had a fantasy that Michael
McGowan was there, bending over her, protecting her.

"Idiot," she murmured.

"Hey," he said softly. "Is that any way to talk to your
brave rescuer?"

Jackie struggled to sit up, but Michael held her down.
"Just lie still a minute. If you don't, you'll probably throw
up when you stand up."

"Gee, thanks," said Jackie, managing a faint smile. "What on earth are you doing here?"

"I was just going to drop in on your friend Marcella. On my way home."

"Aha."

"Don't say aha. It's business. But I heard all kinds of strange noises, and when I got here, Jake was snarling, and your mugger was retreating."

"Did you catch him?"

"No. I didn't even try. I wanted to make sure you were okay."

"Some detective."

"I'll probably get a demotion for this. Dereliction of duty."

Jackie smiled and closed her eyes for a moment. When she opened them again, she had the sense that something was wrong. She tugged urgently at McGowan's sleeve. "Hey, Michael. Where's Jake?"

"He's okay. I moved him inside with Marcella. She's taking care of him."

"What do you mean you moved him? He's hurt?" Jackie sat up sharply. "Ooof!" She grabbed for her head, which had started to throb unbelievably. McGowan tried to hush her, but she was anxious. "Is he okay, Michael?"

"I think so."

"Take me inside." Jackie began to struggle to her feet, her knees wobbling and her posture uncertain. McGowan looked her over carefully. She would probably be okay. No blood anywhere.

"All right." Michael helped her up and, half carrying her, made his way into Marcella's apartment.

"Nurse Jane Fuzzy Wuzzy, the Muskrat Lady, at your service," said Marcella, while Jackie lowered herself groggily onto the sofa. Marcella had made Jake a kind of throne-bed, out of pillows, quilts, and blankets. She had placed a large bowl of water next to him.

"Is he all right?"

"I think so," said Marcella. "He's got a mean gash on his shoulder, and he lost some blood, but he looks fairly alert to me. And his nose is cold."

"Call Jason Huckle," Jackie commanded. "Look him up in the phone book. He lives right around the corner. He's our veterinarian."

McGowan phoned the vet, who turned up, surgical kit under his arm, within a very few minutes. He looked at Jake's wound, gave him a couple of injections, stitched up the cut, and then scowled at Jackie. "Your dog will be fine, Mrs. Walsh. But I understand that there were two mugging victims tonight. Has anybody had a look at you?"

"I'm fine, Dr. Huckle," said Jackie. "Really. Just a little woozy."

"There's a doctor on his way," put in McGowan, who had called Cosmo Gordon. "He'll be here any minute."

"I *really* appreciate your coming, Dr. Huckle," said Jackie.

The veterinarian smiled. He had treated Jake once before, for a gunshot wound. "This dog of yours seems to have a penchant for getting himself involved with violent types, Mrs. Walsh."

"I know. Well, he was just protecting me tonight."

"A good thing too. By the looks of that wound, your attacker meant to kill."

"Meant to kill *Jake*?"

"I would say so." He looked at McGowan. "I think I know you. A cop, right?"

McGowan nodded. "Detective Lieutenant Michael McGowan, at your service."

"Right. And that dog is K-9, if I'm not mistaken."

"That's correct." McGowan flashed a look at Jackie. "Is it that obvious?"

"What's obvious is that he's been trained to avoid lethal attacks. Most dogs would have leapt straight at someone attacking their master or mistress. Mrs. Walsh's dog obviously knew how to avoid the blow. Not altogether, but sufficiently to keep from being killed."

Jason Huckle, after offering a few more insights into Jake's character, gave them instructions not to move him until morning. Then he departed, passing Cosmo Gordon on the stairs on his way out.

"Pleased to have a patient who's still breathing," said the medical examiner, after being briefly apprised of the situation and introduced to Marcella. He bent to peer into Jackie's eyes. "Although strictly from the physiological viewpoint, there isn't all that much difference."

"Thanks," said Jackie, giggling.

He shone a light into her eyes, moved his finger around in the air, tested her reflexes, and gently probed the sore spot on the side of her skull. "I would say that a severe klonk on the head, Jackie, is what you've had."

Marcella laughed. "Please don't use such big words, Doctor."

Gordon grinned. "Yes, a klonk . . . or perhaps a whomp. Lucky for you that Jake here took the knife."

Jackie looked across the room at Jake, who was breathing evenly. The front of his shoulder was swathed in bandages, but otherwise he looked like any dog asleep—contented, lazy, and ready for nothing in particular, except about ten hours more sleep.

"Don't you think it's kind of odd?" asked Jackie.

"What?"

"That my attacker should be content with knocking me out, but decides to pull a knife on Jake."

"Well," said Marcella reasonably, "you're not exactly the same kind of threat as Jake is. So all he needed was to klonk you."

"No." Jackie's voice was assured. "He had to klonk me so he could attack Jake."

"Huh?" said Marcella. "Jackie, I think your brains got scrambled."

She looked from Jackie to McGowan, and from McGowan to Gordon. Neither one of the men spoke.

"Hey." Marcella's nose for news came alive. "What's going on? You guys gonna fill me in?" She folded her arms. "Or," she added, in a voice heavy with irony, "you can just have your little murders and near murders right here in my apartment, and I'll just nurse your dog and won't ask a single question."

"That sounds like a good idea," said Gordon. "It'll be safer for you that way, you see."

For a moment it looked like Marcella would argue. Then she appeared ready to sulk. Finally, however, she took the businesslike approach.

"I get the exclusive, when it's safe to tell."

"But of course," agreed Cosmo amiably, with a look in Jake's direction. "I knew you were a smart one. You get the exclusive when it's safe to tell. Provided, my dear, that there's anyone left to tell it."

CHAPTER 18

Jake and Jackie didn't stir from Marcella's place on Tuesday night. They already knew that the apartment, Marcella had mockingly pointed out, was completely pregnable and totally vulnerable to enterprising burglars. If they wanted to catch their man, they could do it right here. He'd be sure to find a way in.

After everyone's medical needs had been seen to on Tuesday night, Cosmo Gordon left, and McGowan had settled in to ask Marcella more questions about Bambi. Much to Jackie's consternation, Marcella was obliged to reveal the reason she'd even known about Bambi in the first place.

"Um," said Marcella, looking wide-eyed at Jackie, "well, I had suspected the existence of a Bambi all along."

"Yeah—but how did you find her?"

"She found me. She called me, and said, This is Bambi, or something like that."

"And you just guessed that she was Morton Slake's girlfriend."

"Well, yes and no." She glanced at Jackie, who was turning bright red.

"Go on, Marcella. Tell the whole story." Jackie sat back in the sofa and prepared to feel foolish. She was not disappointed. Her escapade in Morton Slake's office sounded even worse when it was related by a third party. She would have fainted from embarrassment, she thought, if only she didn't have such a terrible headache to keep her conscious.

"So," said McGowan, amused. "Jackie was helping you with your story?"

It was time for self-defense. "I was just doing a little investigating, Michael. I happened to be there anyway—"

"You mean that Fred Jackson was there anyway."

"Yes." There was nothing wrong with poking around, her tone implied.

"You're lucky you didn't get caught," said McGowan.

A deep silence descended on the room. Finally, Marcella could contain it no longer, and let out a stifled giggle. It was enough for McGowan.

"Oh, excuse me. You were caught." He gave Jackie an amused stare; then a grin slowly widened on his face. "I know who caught you too!"

"Oh, be quiet, Michael." Jackie blushed a deep, becoming red. Being a free-lance investigator for your friends definitely had its drawbacks.

"What I don't get," said McGowan, "is what Northcote was doing in Slake's office in the first place. They hate each other."

"Are you sure about that?" asked Marcella. She was aware of Jackie's eyes upon her; she was conscious of their discussion, earlier in the evening, about McGowan's antipathy for Northcote. Jackie knew her friend well enough to know that she was fishing for information; she only hoped it wasn't as obvious to Michael McGowan as it was to her.

McGowan admitted that he wasn't sure, actually, that it was just departmental rumor. "But everybody hates Morton Slake. Even his wife."

The two women instantly pressed McGowan for details of the connubial hatred, and were gratified (after Marcella had given her word of honor) by an amusing account of McGowan's visit there. Marcella, of course, had interviewed Marie Zug several times in the course of writing her profile of Slake, but Marie had been nowhere near as forthcoming.

"She showed admirable restraint," said Marcella admiringly. "She could have done a lot of damage if she'd let herself go."

"I thought she *was* letting herself go," said McGowan. "I couldn't get her to turn it off."

After McGowan had finally left, about midnight, Jackie and Marcella had sat up for another hour or so, talking about the Slake mess. The "Dear Slaying," insisted Marcella, was at the root of it all. If only she could get back and talk to Marie Zug again, she would be able to worm it out of her. But Marie had banned all reporters from the premises.

With McGowan gone, Marcella went to work on Jackie to elucidate something concrete about tonight's attack. She was alternately frustrated and angry with her friend for keeping such a promising secret from her, but Jackie reminded Marcella of her own secrecy about the Slake story. In Jackie's mind, they were even.

Jackie was very conscious of the fact that if their suspicions were true—if this attack was aimed at Jake—that Marcella would really be safer if she didn't know anything about it.

Jackie thought long and hard about the events of the night. She didn't really believe that Jake could be used to put a murderer behind bars, but it was becoming clear that someone did think so. And as long as that someone was frightened of Jake—because he had been Matt Dugan's dog, because he had been a witness to the ex-cop's slaying—then Jackie and Peter and Jake were all at risk.

What she needed to do was to hatch a plan to make the murderer's fear work against him.

• • •

By Wednesday evening, Jake's knife wound was healing nicely. It hadn't been deep, after all, and a few stitches and some bedrest had set him right again. He was limping a bit, but Jackie thought he looked handsome and brave. The thick ruff of fur at his neckline hid the small scar that the stitches had left. It looked to Jackie as though the knife had been aimed for his heart. She was gratified, therefore, by the news that McGowan brought with him that evening, when he paid a sympathy call.

"We're convalescing in the den," Jackie told him when she answered the door. "Jake's got a beautiful blanket-lined basket, and I've got the sofa." She led the way to the den, which was really more of a combination library and sun porch. Two walls were lined with bookshelves, interrupted every six feet or so by tall, thin windows. One shelf held a television, video player, and a stereo. There was a huge collection of movies on tape, filed alphabetically by director. An old red leather sofa stood against one wall; on the opposite side of the narrow room there was a fireplace. The room was pretty close to heaven, Jackie thought.

"I think Jake took a chunk out of your attacker last night," he said, reaching down and patting the dog gently. "We found what looks like a shirt cuff and a section of a sleeve. Now all we have to do is look for some joker reporting a dog bite on his arm. Unfortunately, hospitals aren't required to file a report for that. But maybe we'll get lucky."

"Do you think the attacker was after me or after Jake?" she asked McGowan.

He shrugged. "It's impossible to know. Whoever he was, he got you both."

"But admit it, Michael. You think that Jake was the real target." She scowled at him.

"Well—I admit it looks that way. Our guy took the trouble to knock you out with a blackjack or a sock full of marbles—and *then* he pulled a knife."

"Right," she said, nodding. "Was he going to use it on me, as well? Or was he just going to try to hurt Jake?"

"We'll know when we catch him, Jackie. Which we will. I promise you."

Jackie thought about it. She and Peter really relied on Jake, for protection and for companionship. If he himself was a target—and after everything that had happened, Jackie and McGowan both felt this was a possibility—then she and Peter were lost. Jackie and Peter needed Jake to be a pillar of strength for them.

McGowan watched as Jackie's face registered her thoughts.

"It will be over soon, I promise."

"How do you know?"

"Because we're putting the pressure on." McGowan took a seat in a black wooden armchair. The Rodgers University seal was painted in gilt on the back. The chair had belonged to Jackie's father, a graduate of the class of '36.

"There's nothing to be done, Michael. We might as well admit it."

"I don't agree. There's a lot to be done." He gave her a look of intense scrutiny. "Jackie, this is a terribly dangerous game."

"You don't have to tell me that."

"But I do. Jackie, I don't want you trying any of your free-lance investigating into this business of your attack last night. Leave it to the police."

She didn't say anything.

"Look." McGowan's tone was conciliatory. "I would be the first to admit that you've been a great help to me. To the force. But, Jackie, those were cases in which you were not the target. I'm very much afraid that in the present business, your life may be in big danger. You can't sneak up on someone who is already stalking you."

Jackie's face fell. She saw the logic of his argument.

She was not to feel frustrated for long, however. The investigating bug, once stirred up, was difficult to squash. But Jackie simply shifted topics. The mystery surrounding the theft of Marcella's Slake profile—compounded as it had been by the murder of Bambi Wornom—cried out for investigation.

Shortly after Michael left, Nate Northcote called. He expressed dismay at Jackie's adventure. "Mugged? That's awful. Are you all right?"

"I'm fine, thanks. Just mad."

"About what?"

"That I didn't get a better look at the guy. The fog was really heavy, and it happened so fast."

"You'd be amazed at how rarely people can get a good look at someone, when they're taken by surprise," Nate replied. "Courts are clogged with cases, but we don't get as many convictions as we'd like to. Hard to recognize people in moments of stress."

"I suppose so." Jackie thought this conversation was truly strange. She hated it when people lectured you about the statistical implications of your personal experience. She wondered, briefly, if Nate Northcote was just full of hot air. It was beginning to sound that way.

"So—I guess you probably won't be up for our tennis game?"

"Oh." Jackie had forgotten—they had a tennis date for Thursday night. "I think I'll be all right by then. Just don't hit me with a serve or anything."

"Well, the truth is, I'm a wounded soldier myself."

"You are?" This was beginning to sound like a brush-off.

"Yeah. Burned my arm yesterday, trying to light the gas grill. Stupid. But I think I'm out of commission this week."

His arm? On the gas grill? Jackie felt a prickle of fear along her spine.

Jackie brought the conversation to a swift close. She wanted to think about things.

Why had Nate said *recognize*?

She spent several hours trying to put it all out of her mind. Michael was absolutely right—that she had been a target. If the attack had been just a random mugging, no amount of inquiry on her part would help. And if it was targeted—well. It was just much better for the police to handle it.

If she couldn't pursue her own attacker, she could at least pursue the person who had stolen Marcella's notes. She would get to the bottom of the Slake mystery, once and for all. And maybe get a line on Bambi's killer, in the meantime.

Thus Jackie came up with her Red Riding Hood plan—with Jake in the role of the Big Bad Wolf.

CHAPTER 19

On Thursday afternoon, Jackie took Jake to the vet to have his stitches removed. He looked nearly perfect, and he was full of pep, wagging his tail furiously as they left Jason Huckle's office.

The two of them piled in Jackie's Jeep and headed for Lofthill Drive, where Morton Slake lived. The newspaper reports of the Dear Slaying all agreed that Marie Zug had reopened the family portals to her husband, although her motive in so doing was hotly disputed. Some people claimed that she was being nice so Morton would pay her alimony, but others knew that the family money was really all hers, and thought that she just liked the idea of being the mayor's wife. Jackie and Marcella, in talking it over, had agreed that probably Marie Zug didn't want her image to suffer any more than it had to. She had her business to consider, after all, and Morton Slake was the kind of guy, Jackie thought, who would go around bad-mouthing his wife after cheating on her with a Texas blonde called Bambi.

Nobody—except the lone, strident editorial voice of the *Chronicle*, always odd-man-out—seemed to think it remarkable that Morton Slake was still in the running for mayor of Palmer. Only a few members of the present municipal government, and one or two squeaky wheels from the city council, spoke out in public to suggest that Slake's romantic involvement with a young murder victim, not his wife, might unsuit him for civic leadership. It was almost as though he had already won the election.

But obviously, evidently, he had a weak spot. It was clear that there was a chink in the Slake armor—which Jackie thought of as being not so much armor as Scotchgard, a product of modern times. Obviously, there was something wrong with Slake—because otherwise, why would Bambi have been killed?

The police weren't revealing—and neither was Marcella—that Bambi had failed to keep her rendezvous at the Pancake Palace. But Jackie knew that Bambi had been stopped—stopped dead—because she had been about to spill the beans to the local newspaper.

About what? The affair? Then why not Jerry Waters, who paid his "interview" subjects handsomely?

It didn't make any sense, unless you took the position that Bambi had some kind of political dynamite that she was about to use on Slake.

Jackie was going to use the Red Riding Hood method to find out exactly what Bambi had had hidden in her basket of goodies.

While Jackie was approaching the mystery from the fantasy-folklore angle, Michael McGowan was following Marie Zug's advice and using the "Froodian" approach. But instead of psychoanalyzing the victim, he was getting ready to psychoanalyze Margaret Leaming.

He had decided that it would be better to approach Slake's secretary on his own turf. He had therefore sent her a polite note requesting a few moments of her time, at her convenience. She had responded, equally politely, that she had no information whatsoever to offer the police, and therefore she would consider any interview a waste of public resources.

McGowan was deeply amused. He couldn't remember the last time he had come up against such a combination of *lèse-majesté* and sheer nerve. Not in the process of a homicide investigation, at least. Margaret Leaming, he decided, was probably going to be one tough nut to crack.

He straightened his necktie, climbed in his car, and headed for the Municipal Building. When he got there, the short, stubby woman with the rigidly curled, graying hair was just as stubborn as she'd been in her note.

"I see you've come to waste your time with me, despite my message to you, Lieutenant."

"That's right." McGowan pulled a small notebook from his pocket and flipped it open to an empty page. "I'm sure you'll bear with me, Ms. Leaming, even if it all seems pretty dull and boring to you. We like to do things by the book, you know. I'm sure you can appreciate that the methodical approach is sometimes the best."

"If used by a person of intelligence, and in moderation, yes." Margaret Leaming closed a leather-bound desk calendar and sniffed the air. "But now that you're here, it would be folly for you to go away without asking me your questions." She glanced at her watch. It was a Rolex, McGowan noted, with a barely discernible flicker of the eye. "I have ten minutes for you, Lieutenant."

"That'll be plenty." McGowan, at her invitation, seated himself in a leather armchair at the foot of her desk. "Since you have nothing to contribute, Ms. Leaming, may I take it that you never knew the dead woman?"

"I met her on one or two occasions, when our paths happened to cross here at the office."

"What did you think of her?"

"I didn't bother to form an opinion of her."

"Mind if I ask why?"

"Not at all. Lieutenant, Morton Slake is the president of the Palmer city council. I don't consider adulterous affairs to be consistent with his level of responsibility in government. My feeling is that everyone has his weak points—but that it is far, far better never to give in to them, if possible. You only make yourself vulnerable."

"To what?"

The question seemed to surprise Margaret Leaming. She thought for a moment. "To defeat."

"You think that Slake became a less effective councilman because of his affair?"

"No."

"Then where was the harm in it?"

"The harm lies in giving way to impulses that betray your trust—whether it is the trust of shareholders, a spouse, or a city. It was not in Morton's best interests to appear to be someone capable of betraying a solemn trust."

McGowan was silent for a moment. "Ever meet Mrs. Slake? That is, Marie Zug?"

"Yes, of course. I have been Morton's confidential secretary for twenty-three years. Marie and I have known each other a long time."

"She has quite a strong opinion about you."

"About me?"

"Yes, ma'am. She says Morton"—he flipped momentarily through his notes—"'couldn't wipe his nose' if you weren't there to tell him where it is."

Margaret Leaming's face remained unchanged. "That's an interesting point of view."

"In fact, what Marie Zug thinks—as an insider, but not as a politician—is that you're pretty much running the show here for Morton Slake."

"A secretary's job can sometimes seem that way, Lieutenant."

"Would you agree that you are the effective force behind Morton Slake?"

"I would agree that I have a certain amount to say about what he does in his role of city council president."

"Yet he defied you, and persisted in his affair with Ms. Wornom."

"I wouldn't call it defiance."

"What would you call it?"

"Exercising bad taste and bad judgment."

"If he'd had a different *kind* of mistress—someone prominent, wealthy, who might have helped his career?"

She hesitated. "That's an absurd question."

"I'm only looking for your opinion here, Ms. Leaming. You see, the impression I'm getting—and it's a strong one, no doubt about it—is that you considered Bambi Wornom to be bad for Morton Slake's future. She was, ipso facto, bad for your future. It was imperative, therefore, that you get her out of the way. Morton Slake had defied you, and made you very angry—oh, I forgot to mention that we have a witness to a quarrel you had with him, the day before she was killed."

"What on earth are you talking about?" Margaret Leaming had gone pale.

"We have had a long conversation with Timothy Falloes."

An ugly reddish-purple suffused Margaret Leaming's pasty complexion. She said nothing, however.

"And he has given us a statement about a message that you took, ostensibly from Bambi, purporting to say that she couldn't make a date."

"I never took any such message. Ask Morton."

"I have. He says that he thinks you *did* take that message, but for some reason you didn't want to admit it."

McGowan rested an ankle across a knee and looked at Margaret Leaming with a casualness that hid the intensity of his scrutiny. He knew thanks to his conversation with Jackie and Marcella, that it was Jackie who had taken the message. But Margaret Leaming didn't know that. He would use the issue like a crowbar. "Was that perhaps because you were making arrangements of your own? To get rid of Bambi?"

"I would like to call my attorney," said Margaret Leaming.

Out at the Slake house, the Red Riding Hood approach was not really going according to plan. Jackie, in her excitement, hadn't bothered to ask Michael McGowan if Marie Zug had dogs—and if so, how many, and of what type and disposition. It was a foolish oversight, and it threatened to render her whole marvelous plan utterly useless.

Jackie's plan was fairly complex—but then, she'd had two days of recovering from her concussion in which to think it all up. She thought it was brilliant—and based on the impression of Marie Zug that she'd gotten from Michael, she was pretty sure it might work.

Her idea was that she and Marcella would drive out together. Marcella would wait in the car (so as not to be recognized by Marie Zug) while Jackie put her plan into action. Jackie was going to pose as a volunteer from the Palmer Pet Pals, a local not-for-profit animal hospital, with Jake as a prop. She was raising money for improvements to the new animal shelter, but what the fund drive really needed was a little zing, a little zip. So she had come, as a representative of PPP, to ask Marie's help. Wouldn't she be willing to contribute her talents to designing a recipe for a gourmet Doggy Treat? They would market the Treats according to her strict specifications (at no cost to herself, of course), and all of the profits would go to the PPP. Marie, of course, would reap a small licensing fee; she would also be in for a great deal of free publicity, on PPP posters throughout the greater Palmer area.

Once inside the kitchen—with its tables covered with bows and gold paint and baskets and rickrack—Jackie would just sit and listen to Marie's conversation, guiding it ever so gently toward the subject that she wanted to probe—who, or what, was Slake really afraid of?

In the meantime, Marcella could snoop around a little bit. She might run into some helpers, on their way to or from gathering pinecones. Or she might get some information out of the servants. Jackie would just be sure to keep Marie Zug occupied for a full half hour, while Marcella did what she could.

Jackie thought it was brilliant. Marcella agreed that it had possibilities. The only thing that neither of them had reckoned on was corgis.

These were no ordinary corgis—not a cute little pair or threesome like the Queen and the Queen Mother have, but close to a score of them. When Jackie pulled up in the driveway, they swarmed the car, like outer space creatures in a sci-fi flick. Jake, unable to restrain himself, set up a furious barking, and began to hurl himself at the window. The Jeep rocked with the violence of Jake's movements, but Jackie was afraid to drive away. She had no idea how many corgis there were—it had been impossible to count them when they first swarmed the car, and because they were such low-down dogs, there was no telling if there might be some stuck under the chassis.

So Jackie did the only thing she could think of. She leaned on the horn, and honked like mad, and hoped desperately to be delivered from the corgis.

CHAPTER 20

Corky Dole, Margaret Leaming's lawyer, arrived in her office in no time flat. Tall, blond, well built, and well spoken, he was familiar to McGowan—but not from the courtroom. Corky Dole managed most of the real-estate legal work for Slake Properties. That made him the single most important real-estate lawyer in all of Palmer. Corky Dole was a quiet man, but an extraordinarily powerful one, with every bank and business in the city beholden to him in some way.

This was not what McGowan needed.

"Now, what's all this?" asked Dole, after shaking hands, man-to-man. His attitude was smooth—perfectly designed to show that while McGowan wasn't one of the Brotherhood, he was still entitled to a modicum of respect. Until Dole changed his mind, at least. He had an attack mode that could be at least as vicious as Jake's.

"Mr. Dole, I'm sure you know what brings a lieutenant of homicide to see Ms. Leaming."

"Oh, that girl who got herself murdered. Did you catch the fellow yet?"

"No. I was hoping that your client might be able to help us out with that."

"How so?" Dole took a seat, smoothing out the knees

of his trousers and looking at McGowan with wide-eyed interest. His conservative blue suit, white shirt, and rep tie masked a willingness to approach problems with an unorthodox ferocity, McGowan knew.

Patiently McGowan explained what had brought him here. The argument about Bambi Wornom that Falloes had reported, in all its lurid detail. Margaret Leaming sat quite still, uttering not a sound, while McGowan went through the whole tale again.

When he had finished, Dole raised an eyebrow. "Margaret?"

"The whole thing is absurd," she said with asperity. "I had no reason to murder that girl."

"Who said you murdered her?" asked Dole, a cautionary gleam in his eyes.

"I think it ought to be clear that I stayed as far away from her, and from the subject of Morton's girlfriends, as was humanly possible."

McGowan pricked up his ears at the word "girlfriends." Bambi could be just the tip of the iceberg, so to speak, he realized. His heart sank. They would have to try to trace them all. It would take months. Years.

"I think that was a very wise policy," Corky Dole was saying, his voice soft and reasonable. "And I think—if I know my police—that all the good lieutenant here cares about is getting to the bottom of this case." He stood up and adjusted his conservative blue suit. "Where's this Falloes?"

"God," said Margaret. "Out at Morton's house."

"What's he doing out there?"

"Nobody could get anything done here. Too much commotion. So Morton suggested they go out there, go over some papers, who knows what. If you ask me, it's just a plain, old-fashioned council of war."

"Well, then," suggested Corky Dole smoothly. "Shall we join them?"

The odd trio made its way out to Morton Slake's house in McGowan's department-issue Ford, which had been parked right out front of the Municipal Building. "The parking is the only perk we get," he said, trying to sound friendly. "I try to take advantage of it whenever possible."

From the back seat, Corky Dole grunted. "There are times when I feel I'd give a year's salary to have that perk."

"I'll let you borrow my car sometime," joked McGowan.

They rode the rest of the way in silence.

Nothing could have prepared them for the sight that greeted their eyes when they entered Morton Slake's driveway. For a moment it seemed to McGowan as though a miniature herd of cattle had somehow got on the loose. The noise, however, was clearly canine, and it took him only a stunned half second to recognize Jackie's red Jeep. The Jeep was rocking back and forth as Jake threw himself violently from one side to another. In the front seats, Jackie and Marcella were laughing and blowing the horn.

"Good heavens!" exclaimed Margaret Leaming. It was the first utterance she'd made in twenty minutes.

Everything happened at once. It took less than five minutes, really, to sort out the corgi mess, but in her embarrassed amusement, it seemed to Jackie that it had taken hours. The whole thing would have been hilarious, except for one minor detail—it would have to be Michael McGowan to the rescue again!

Margaret Leaming showed characteristic presence of mind. In a flash she was out of McGowan's car, striding toward the Jeep like some laird who's found a poacher on his moors. She bent forward slightly, stared at the captives of the Jeep, and marched toward the front door.

Morton Slake, a hangdog look on his face, slouched out a few moments later. He was followed by some kind of manservant, who—with a whistle—rounded up the corgis and herded them into a small corral at the back of the garage. Jackie tried to count them as they scurried off to their quarters—it seemed to her to be seventeen, but in the seething mass of dog hide it was impossible to tell if she had missed some.

McGowan glared at her, then headed on inside with Margaret Leaming and Corky Dole. The front door shut behind them with a bang.

Jake drooped his head over the back of the seat and let out a low whine.

"Whew!" said Marcella, winding down her windows. "We need a little fresh air. Jake, you have bad breath," she told the dog.

"Marcella?"

"What?"

"Why didn't you tell me that the Slakes have a hundred and fifty-two dogs?" Jackie rolled down her window, gulping for air. Jake's breath, it had to be admitted, was *not* the freshest.

"I didn't know."

"I thought you said you'd been out here ten times?"

"I have. But the dogs weren't loose then."

"One corgi is fine. Even two or three are cute. But a hundred and fifty-two are just disgusting."

"She's a woman of excesses."

"You think the dogs are hers?"

"Oh. Yeah—they're definitely hers. Morton Slake has really bad allergies to dogs."

"Then why does his wife have seventeen of them?"

"You're asking me?"

The two women waited in silence to see if they could learn the outcome of McGowan's mysterious trip to the Slake house. Jackie and Marcella both knew that something good had to be going on. Marcella had recognized Corky Dole as the Slake Properties lawyer. "He's no Perry Mason, but he's definitely a mover and a shaker," she reflected, enumerating the dollar value of his annual services to Slake Properties. "I bet he'll make poor Michael feel pretty powerless."

"I wouldn't bet on it," said Jackie. There was a hint of pride in her voice. She was pleased that Michael was brave enough to come out here to the Slake house on his own. He could easily have asked for intervention from Max Greenaway.

The thought of Greenaway turned Jackie's mind to Nate Northcote. She looked at Marcella.

"Nate and I were supposed to play tennis tonight," she said. "At the Morrell Courts."

"Doesn't look like it's going to rain," replied Marcella, puzzled. "Your head still hurting you?"

"No. Nate's the one with the injury. He hurt his arm."

"How?"

"Told me something about burning it."

"Let me guess," said Marcella, realization beginning to dawn. "You don't believe him."

"Oh, I believe him, all right. It's just that I don't think he burned himself. I think he got bitten by a dog." She reached behind her and scratched Jake's ear. "Good boy." She turned to Marcella. "Let's just get out of this car."

"Think it's safe?"

"If those dogs could get out, they'd have been here by now." In the distance they could hear the continued, concerted barking of the corgis. "If the master is allergic, I bet they have a pretty secure gate."

"Right."

Both women opened their doors. Jackie put Jake on his lead and let him out to sniff at some bushes. "Good boy, Jake." She looked at Marcella. "Burned his arm."

The front door opened, and Margaret Leaming was the first to step out into the sunshine. There was a small adjustment to her expression—you couldn't call it a smile, really, it was more of an adjustment. But Jackie could see at once that Margaret Leaming was happier than she had been. Next came Corky Dole, looking successful. But Corky Dole, and those like him, always look successful. They have to.

Morton Slake came out and stood on the front step. He didn't appear to notice the two strange women standing on his front lawn, although Margaret Leaming was beginning to frown in their direction. Where was Michael?

Another figure stepped out onto the lawn, and began to walk with the group toward Michael's car.

"Who's that?" asked Marcella, squinting.

"The junior bodyguard."

"Oh—the one who was at the council meeting. Right." Marcella studied Tim Falloes as he approached. When he was about ten yards away, Marcella stiffened.

Jackie looked at her friend, then at Falloes, and then back at Marcella.

There was something wrong with the picture. What was it? And where was Michael? Jackie gave Jake's lead a nervous tug, dragging his reluctant nose from beneath a rhododendron.

Jake turned, took one look at Falloes, and all hell broke loose.

The lead was ripped from Jackie's hand, and in less than four seconds, Jake had Tim Falloes pinned helpless to the ground. Margaret Leaming was rooted to the spot with terror. The sound of Jake's vicious snarling brought Michael, at last, from the house, followed by the sound of a woman's voice saying a long and none-too-specific farewell. Marie Zug, thought Jackie.

One look at the scene on the lawn brought Michael running. He glared at Jackie. "Call your dog off, for God's sake," he ordered harshly.

Jackie was transfixed by the sight of Falloes's right arm, where Jake had ripped his shirt. It was swathed in bandages.

"I don't think so," replied Jackie.

Jake, snarling quietly, stood careful watch over Falloes, who hadn't moved a muscle since he'd been tackled.

"Jackie!" McGowan looked furiously at her.

"No—she's right, Michael," said Marcella. She was still staring at Falloes. "I think, if you do a little research, you'll find out that this is someone you're interested in. Well, if you're not, the Philadelphia police are. Mickey Farrow, I think, was the name he was using there."

"Huh?"

Marcella rolled her eyes and looked down at Falloes. "I know you," she said. "You used to be a bag man for big Bill Curtis, right?"

Falloes squirmed. "Get him *off*!" The words came out in a harsh, terrified croak.

"And when Curtis didn't want you anymore, you went over to the other side. As a hit man. But not a very good one. Am I right?"

"Argh, lady, get this dog—"

Jackie felt a thrill of intuition run through her. All of a sudden, she felt very calm. Jake was at a point where he could go either way—but Jackie knew that he would do as she bade him. She spoke up.

"Michael, this is the man that tried to kill Jake the other night."

"Get your dog off me, lady!"

"And I would bet you anything, Michael," Jackie continued, "that he knows something about who killed Matt Dugan. Because just look at Jake. He hates this man."

"Get him off!"

"He hates you, you know." Jackie's voice was quiet, and an eerie calm had settled over all of the gathered spectators. It was as strange and horrible a sight as most of them would ever see—that dog, desperate for the blood of the man pinned beneath his sturdy feet. Jake had never looked more like a killer.

"Just look at him," said Jackie.

CHAPTER 21

Jake, for all his fury, was an exceptionally well-trained dog. At the first word of command, he had backed off from Falloes—but by that time, Michael McGowan had plenty of information to work with.

It took the Palmer police department, in conjunction with the office of the prosecuting attorney, just three weeks to get the indictments they needed.

Tim Falloes, in the hope of beating a murder charge, opened up an extremely dirty bag of tricks to please the prosecutor. Names, mostly, of people in the city government who had been touched by the mob; ways in which they'd been vulnerable.

Bambi, it turned out, had been a shill. It had been clear to some of the big boys for a long time that Morton Slake had a soft spot. Bambi was a plant; once she had him over a barrel, he was obliged to give Falloes a job. The idea had been to push Margaret Leaming out of the way—if Slake was going to be anyone's puppet, it would be under the watchful eye of Bill Curtis, the underworld boss in Palmer. Curtis would tell Slake what his policies were—on gun control and everything else.

Margaret was the one, of course, who explained to him the possibility of being an accessory after the fact in Bambi's murder. Once he understood the position, Morton Slake opened up like a snapping turtle's mouth at feeding time. He confirmed what Falloes hinted, and Falloes confirmed what Slake had only suspected. The mob had been systematically moving in on Palmer city government.

Marcella got her scoop, this time without any interference from those who had a vested interest in Slake's victory on Election Day.

Slake, afraid of reprisals, took advantage of the government's witness protection program; but Marie Zug, of course, was far too well known for that. She declined politely, saying she was sure that nobody would bother her. In fact, nobody did bother her. She continued to live in the big house, all alone, taking in huge monthly shipments of freezer paper and pinecones.

Nate Northcote cut quite an impressive figure at some of the trials—although his impressiveness had more to do with his good looks than with his performance. He sat suavely at the prosecutors' table, taking notes, although most of the charges were federal ones, and he had no real role to play. Still, he looked good—handsome as ever; and when Tim Falloes was brought to trial for the murders of Bambi Wornom and Matt Dugan, Jackie felt sure that Nate would shine.

She waved to him politely on those days when she could sneak away from school and head downtown to the trials. She had seen him, actually, the day after Falloes's arrest, because she had come downtown to give evidence. He had been surprised to see her. His arm? His arm was fine.

Jackie found out later, through Max Greenaway, that Northcote had been lying about having burned his arm. Northcote, in fact, had dinner with the Greenaways that night, and he had brought another woman with him.

"A deep flaw in the psyche," said Marcella.

On the first Tuesday in November, Jackie and Peter made dinner for McGowan, Cosmo and Nancy Gordon, and Marcella Jacobs. They ate in the den (as a special treat) so that they could watch the election returns. Peter, now in the sixth grade, drank root beer with his spaghetti. The rest of the merry party drank red wine, and plenty of it. They were celebrating the landslide victory of Jane Bellamy in the race for mayor. She had announced, in the spirit of continuity, that she intended to keep Margaret Leaming on as a special adviser on municipal affairs.

"Smart move," said Gordon.

They drank a toast to Jane Bellamy.

Michael McGowan had a few other things to celebrate, as well.

Evan Stillman, he told Jackie with a smile, had been given a dishonorable discharge.

"Don't be modest, Michael," insisted Cosmo Gordon, "tell the folks what else."

"What, Cosmo?" asked Jackie as Michael began to show signs of self-consciousness.

"That's Captain McGowan there. As of today."

There were cheers and toasts all around. Jake, unable to resist the excitement, loped into the den and looked from one to the next, as they drank a toast—first to Michael, then to Marcella, then to Jackie, then to Peter, then to Cosmo and Nancy.

When they were finished with their toasts, Jackie said, "Haven't we forgotten someone?"

They looked at her, and she raised her glass. "To Matt Dugan, a hell of a good cop."

Michael McGowan, in an impulsive moment, leaned over and gave her a big kiss. "We forgot someone else," he said.

Jake wagged his tail and let out with a large *woof!* of approval as they all raised their glasses to him.

—————— **MYSTERY'S BRIGHT NORTHERN LIGHT** ——————

DANA STABENOW

Even a blizzard can't cover up the tracks of criminals fast enough to fool Investigator Kate Shugak. This Alaskan ex-District Attorney is always one step ahead of trouble. Possessing brains, guts, and a great respect for Alaskan traditions, she's one detective who doesn't keep her head buried in the snow.

___*A COLD DAY FOR MURDER* 0-425-13301-X/$3.99

With her loyal Husky, savvy investigator Kate Shugak goes back to her roots in the far Alaskan north...where the murder of a National Park Ranger puts her detecting skills to the test.

"Compelling, brutal and true." —*The Boston Globe*
"An enjoyable and well-written yarn." —*Publishers Weekly*

___*A FATAL THAW* 0-425-13577-2/$3.99

Kate Shugak and her Husky, Mutt, must uncover some old hatreds before the murderer of a golden blonde with a tarnished past melts into the Alaskan snowscape.

___*DEAD IN THE WATER* 0-425-13749-X/$3.99

Kate goes undercover, working on a crab fishing boat to try to find out why its obnoxious crew is now mysteriously shrinking.

For Visa, MasterCard and American Express ($15 minimum) orders call: 1-800-631-8571

FOR MAIL ORDERS: CHECK BOOK(S). FILL OUT COUPON. SEND TO:

BERKLEY PUBLISHING GROUP
390 Murray Hill Pkwy., Dept. B
East Rutherford, NJ 07073

NAME _____

ADDRESS _____

CITY _____

STATE _____ ZIP _____

PLEASE ALLOW 6 WEEKS FOR DELIVERY.
PRICES ARE SUBJECT TO CHANGE WITHOUT NOTICE.

POSTAGE AND HANDLING:
$1.75 for one book, 75¢ for each additional. Do not exceed $5.50.

BOOK TOTAL $ ____

POSTAGE & HANDLING $ ____

APPLICABLE SALES TAX $ ____
(CA, NJ, NY, PA)

TOTAL AMOUNT DUE $ ____

PAYABLE IN US FUNDS.
(No cash orders accepted.)

441

DEADLY DEEDS AND SUPER SLEUTHS

___**ONE FOR THE MONEY by D.B. Borton** 1-55773-869-6/$4.50

After thirty-eight years of marriage, Catherine "Cat" Caliban's life has changed: she lost a husband, got a gun, and decided to become a P.I. And that's before she discovered that her upstairs apartment came furnished...with a corpse. Watch for the next Cat Caliban mystery, *Two Points for Murder*, in 10/93.

___**SING A SONG OF DEATH by Catherine Dain**

0-515-11057-4/$3.99

When she's not with her cats, flying her plane, or playing Keno, Reno's Freddie O'Neal is cracking mystery cases. The odds are on Freddie to discover who really lowered the curtain on the hottest lounge act in Lake Tahoe.

___**DOG COLLAR CRIME by Melissa Cleary** 1-55773-896-3/$3.99

Jackie Walsh and her ex-police dog, Jake, are going undercover at a dog-training academy, where the owner was strangled with a choke chain. Since the only two witnesses are basset hounds, it's up to Jackie and Jake to collar the culprit. Watch for the next Dog Lover's mystery, *Hounded to Death*, in 9/93.

___**MRS. JEFFRIES DUSTS FOR CLUES by Emily Brightwell**

0-425-13704-X/$3.99

A servant girl is missing...along with a valuable brooch. When Inspector Witherspoon finds the brooch on the body of a murdered woman, one mystery is solved—but another begins. Fortunately, Mrs. Jeffries, his housekeeper, isn't the sort to give up on a case before every loose end is tightly tied.

___**BROADCAST CLUES by Dick Belsky** 0-425-11153-8/$4.50

Television reporter Jenny McKay covers the story of a missing bride-to-be in a high society wedding and uncovers a stash of family secrets, high profile lowlifes, political scandal and unanswered questions.

___**FAT-FREE AND FATAL by Jaqueline Girdner**

1-55773-917-X/$3.99

Marin County detective Kate Jasper signs up for a vegetarian cooking class. Instead of learning the fine art of creating meatless main dishes, Kate gets a lesson on murder when one of the students is choked to death.

For Visa, MasterCard and American Express ($15 minimum) orders call: 1-800-631-8571

FOR MAIL ORDERS: CHECK BOOK(S). FILL OUT COUPON. SEND TO:

BERKLEY PUBLISHING GROUP
390 Murray Hill Pkwy., Dept. B
East Rutherford, NJ 07073

NAME_____

ADDRESS_____

CITY_____

STATE_____ ZIP_____

PLEASE ALLOW 6 WEEKS FOR DELIVERY.
PRICES ARE SUBJECT TO CHANGE WITHOUT NOTICE.

POSTAGE AND HANDLING:
$1.75 for one book, 75¢ for each additional. Do not exceed $5.50.

BOOK TOTAL	$ _____
POSTAGE & HANDLING	$ _____
APPLICABLE SALES TAX (CA, NJ, NY, PA)	$ _____
TOTAL AMOUNT DUE	$ _____

PAYABLE IN US FUNDS.
(No cash orders accepted.)